Tried & True

LOOK FOR THE OTHER BOOKS IN THIS
inspirational series from BANTAM BOOKS.

SPECIAL EDITION
The Diaries

COMING SOON:
#17 Just Say Yes

clearwater crossing

Tried & True

laura peyton roberts

BANTAM BOOKS
NEW YORK • TORONTO • LONDON • SYDNEY • AUCKLAND

RL 5.8, age 12 and up
TRIED & TRUE
A Bantam Book/December 2000

ISBN: 0-553-49331-0

Visit us on the Web! www.randomhouse.com/teens
Educators and librarians, for a variety of teaching tools, visit us at
www.randomhouse.com/teachers

Published simultaneously in the United States and Canada

Bantam Books is an imprint of Random House Children's Books, a
division of Random House, Inc. BANTAM BOOKS and the rooster
colophon are registered trademarks of Random House, Inc.
Bantam Books, 1540 Broadway, New York, New York 10036.

PRINTED IN THE UNITED STATES OF AMERICA

OPM   10 9 8 7 6 5 4 3 2 1

Above all else, guard your heart, for it is the wellspring of life.

Proverbs 4:23

One

"I'm home!" Nicole Brewster announced, slamming her family's front door after school on Friday. She headed for the stairway quickly, before her mother could get any bright ideas about inventing extra chores, but she wasn't fast enough to beat her younger sister, Heather.

"You're late," Heather said, running out of the kitchen. Her blond hair hung in unwashed strings, and her shirt was totally wrong with her pants. "Why are you so late?"

"I had something to do," Nicole returned haughtily, brushing past the eighth-grader to reach the bottom stair. "Not that it's any of your business," she added on the way up.

"You're the one who said we were going shopping for Mom's present this afternoon," Heather retorted, right on her heels. "You promised! And now it's practically dinnertime."

"Oh."

She *had* said that. But that was nearly a week ago, way before she'd known that Melanie Andrews was

1

going to drop out of the cheerleading squad and make a place for her. Obviously, getting measured for her cheerleading uniform had immediately become Nicole's new top priority. She had just arrived home from rushing downtown with her deposit check, completely forgetting about the Mother's Day gift she had planned to chip in on with Heather.

Reaching her bedroom, Nicole pushed the door open, Heather sticking to her like a bad reputation.

"So *now* what are we going to do?" the little pest demanded. "Mom is never going to let us go this close to dinner."

"We'll go tomorrow. There'll be plenty of time, I promise."

"You promised *this* time."

"Well, excuse me, but I've been a *little* busy, Heather. You're too young to understand."

Nicole pushed her sister out into the hallway, shutting the door in her face before she could react.

"Understand what?" Heather shouted through the wood. "I understand you've been a total pain in the neck ever since you made cheerleader! You think you're so great, but you're exactly the same, Nicole!"

"Yeah, yeah. Go squeeze a zit or something."

Heather sputtered on the other side of the door, finally kicking it before retreating to her own room.

She's such a baby, Nicole thought, tossing her backpack onto her bed. *Then again, what can I expect from a thirteen-year-old?*

Heather couldn't possibly comprehend the magnitude of Nicole's rise in status since she'd been added to the CCHS cheerleading squad. Nicole could barely comprehend it herself. Two afternoons before, when she'd found out Melanie had relinquished her place on the squad, it was almost as if Nicole's life had started over. She was *somebody* now—and as soon as word of her new position got out to the rest of the students, she'd *really* be somebody.

Maybe in the fall, when Heather—heaven forbid—started high school, she'd finally understand. In fact, if Heather played her cards right, she might even benefit from her big sister's popularity. But until then . . .

What was Melanie thinking? Nicole wondered for the hundredth time as she flopped down on her bed. Not that she wasn't grateful. *Still, a person has to be crazy to voluntarily drop the squad.*

Nicole remembered the conversation they'd had about it just a few minutes after she'd first heard the news.

"Did you leave the squad for me?" she had demanded, catching up with Melanie outside the library. Her chest had been heaving, both from the excitement of the cheerleading coach's announcement and from dread that Melanie would say the whole thing had been a mistake. "Don't say you did it for me," she had begged, "because how will I ever pay you back?"

Melanie had shrugged and pushed her tawny hair off her forehead, her light green eyes as inscrutable as always. "You don't need to pay me back. Besides, I can always try out for the squad again as a senior. Or maybe Sandra will even put me back on for next year, if someone else drops out. Anything could happen between now and then."

"I just . . . I wish you were on it now. With me," Nicole had said, feeling slightly guilty. "You're going to miss camp, and I just . . . just . . ." She'd trailed off, at a loss. "Thank you," she'd finally added, realizing that was what she should have said in the first place.

"You're welcome," Melanie had returned with a smile. "But don't be surprised if cheerleading isn't everything you expect. I mean, it's fun and all. Just don't expect it to change your life."

Staring at her bedroom ceiling now, Nicole remembered those words clearly. What had Melanie been talking about? Of *course* it was going to change her life!

Cheerleading is just like modeling, only better, because all the people who see me will be people from school. I'm going to be so popular next year! It's completely inevitable.

Her only regret was that her good fortune had come at her friend's expense. Not only that, but Melanie had made Nicole promise never to tell the cheerleading coach, Sandra Kincaid, or any of the girls the real reason for her abrupt departure.

"Sandra might not like it if she knew, and it's nobody else's business," Melanie had said. "Things will be smoother all the way around if we keep this to ourselves."

Nicole agreed. Even so, *she* knew the truth—and it bugged her.

"I'm just not going to think about it anymore," she announced loudly, sitting up on her bed. "Melanie's a big girl. She knew what she was doing. Besides, feeling bad takes all the fun out of it."

And it had to be wrong not to enjoy such a fabulous, unexpected gift. It might even seem ungrateful if she didn't take full advantage of the opportunity Melanie had provided.

Nicole smiled. *No one needs to worry about that. I'm going to milk being a cheerleader for everything it's worth!*

Jenna Conrad burst out the passenger door of Peter Altmann's Toyota almost before the car had stopped, full of excitement about the Saturday CPR class she had come to take with Eight Prime. The cars already parked and deserted told her she and Peter were the last to arrive at the lake, and she practically bolted for the trailhead leading to the Junior Explorers' summer day camp site.

"Where are you getting your energy?" Peter teased behind her. "Didn't all those kids hanging on you at the park wear you out?"

"Not at all!" she said happily, full of her good mood. "Besides, when we're camp counselors, we'll have kids hanging on us all day. Helping out with the Explorers this morning was just the thing to get me in shape."

"They'd better not hang on *me* all day," said Peter, catching up to her on the leaf-strewn path. "You shouldn't let kids use your arms like closet poles—it only makes them whiny."

"They just want a little attention."

"If you say so. I *guess* I'll still love you when your hands swing down past your knees."

"You guess?" she giggled, pushing him up the trail. "You'd better!"

Peter shook his head uncertainly, blond bangs twitching over laughing blue eyes. "I dunno. We'll have to see."

"All right for you, then," Jenna returned, skipping ahead of him on the path. The trees overhead were bursting with green, and birds sang from their branches. "Last one to CPR is a rotten egg!"

She took off at a sprint, her long hair flying, hoping to use the element of surprise and the narrowness of the path to keep Peter stuck behind her. Her strategy worked until just before the packed-dirt clearing, where the trail widened out like a funnel. Peter blew past her in the final section, reaching the clearing first.

"Ha!" He threw his hands overhead and did a victory dance. "You should have pushed with those ape arms the kids stretched out for you."

"Peter!" she squealed, chasing him across the clearing toward the camp's new flagpole. The pine-green cabin Eight Prime had refurbished sat in the shade of the woods to her left, but all the other members of the group had gravitated to the long split-log benches beneath the flagpole. Melanie and Nicole had seats on the first bench, next to Ben Pipkin, and Leah Rosenthal and Miguel del Rios reclined on the second with Jesse Jones. Traci Evans, their twenty-something instructor, was nowhere to be seen, though, and Jenna felt a rush of relief. She and Peter might be last, but at least they weren't late.

"Hey, everyone," said Jenna, abandoning the chase to trot up to the benches. "No sign of Traci yet?"

"Nope." Melanie flicked a bug off one slender arm. "What are you two so smiley about?"

"Junior Explorers. You should have seen how cute the kids were this morning. They're so excited about starting camp in a couple of weeks."

"Is Elton coming?" Ben asked, naming the little boy Jenna knew was his favorite.

"Yes. And Amy, and Jason," she answered, adding Melanie's and Jesse's. "I can't *wait* for summer! Sarah's physical therapist is going to have her start

7

swimming when school gets out, and Caitlin said she would drive her up here to the lake sometimes, when she doesn't have to work."

Jenna stopped talking long enough to flash Peter a smile. Ever since Sarah had almost been killed by a drunk driver, all the Conrad girls had gone out of their way to spoil their youngest sister. But Jenna also knew that spending free hours hauling Sarah to the lake would be no hardship for Caitlin, who could hardly wait for Peter's older brother, David, to come home from college and start supervising the Junior Explorers' day camp.

"Traci is coming," Jesse said, pointing toward the trailhead. "It's about time we got this show on the road."

Jenna turned to see Traci struggling into the clearing, an armless mannequin torso under each arm and a heavy-looking canvas bag slung by a strap across her chest. Peter and Miguel ran off to help their CPR instructor, relieving her of a dummy apiece.

"We should get these spread out," Leah said. She stood and started flapping a blue plastic tarp with both hands, trying to cover a square of the level ground in front of the benches.

Jenna hurried to grab another blue tarp off the bench, and Nicole pitched in with a third made of green canvas. With Melanie's help, the girls laid the tarps end to end, and a moment later the guys dropped the mannequins onto them. Traci's canvas

8

bag thudded down last, barely missing her own dusty sneaker.

"Whew, that's a hike!" she said, huffing to catch her breath. "It didn't seem that far when I came out here last time."

"Maybe because all you were carrying then were those little first-aid booklets," Jenna suggested.

"Maybe." Traci smoothed her short dark hair away from her flushed cheeks. "I'll definitely get some help with this stuff on the way back out."

"These dummies are so cool!" Ben said, dropping onto his knees for a closer look. "Except . . . why don't they have faces?"

"They do. They're in here." Unzipping her canvas bag, Traci began passing out floppy rubber masks to each member of Eight Prime. "When it's your turn for mouth-to-mouth, you attach your own rubber face to the mannequin. Then afterwards I'll take them all back to be sterilized. Things stay a little more sanitary that way."

"Eew," Nicole said, curling one glossy lip. "You mean somebody else's mouth was on this?"

Jenna looked dubiously at the slab of putty-colored rubber in her hands, while Jesse pulled his on over his own features.

"Somebody *kiss* me!" he said, in a not-bad Jim Carrey imitation.

Melanie and Nicole giggled. Ben started to stand up.

"Not you, Ben!" Jesse said, hurriedly ripping the mask from his face.

"I wasn't going to!" Ben protested.

"I will," said Miguel, batting his brown eyes at Jesse.

Peter cracked up.

"All right. If everybody's done goofing around . . ." Traci looked at each member of the group, a little impatiently. "I hope you all remembered to bring your first-aid booklets from last time, because the CPR information is in there too."

"We were supposed to *bring* those?" Nicole said. "You never told us that!"

"Yes, she did," Jenna said. "She told us like five times."

Nicole looked unconvinced. "I never heard it."

"You can share with me," Jenna said, taking her own, slightly battered booklet out of her back jeans pocket.

"I don't have mine, either," said Jesse.

"Me either," said Melanie.

"Wasn't *anybody* listening?" Jenna asked irritably.

People stared, but she didn't care. It was embarrassing to appear so unprepared in front of Traci, especially when they were all supposedly mature enough to be counselors. Before that they had to get their certificates, though, which meant they not only had to pass CPR, they still had to take a major water safety class. They didn't have time to be lame.

10

"Here, Jenna, let Nicole and Melanie use your book, and you can look on with me," Peter said, quickly taking charge. "Leah, how about lending yours to Jesse and sharing with Miguel?"

The booklets got shuffled around, and soon everyone was seated cross-legged on the tarps, ready to give Traci their full attention.

There. You got all excited for nothing, Jenna reprimanded herself, trying to normalize her breathing. On the other hand, if she had overreacted a little it wasn't *totally* her own fault. Between Nicole's personal problems and Ben's endless anecdotes, first-aid class hadn't gone smoothly, and CPR covered even more material. If people didn't start getting serious . . .

"Don't worry," Peter leaned over to whisper, somehow reading her mind. "We'll get through this. Piece of cake."

She gave him a reluctant smile. Maybe she was being too much of a perfectionist.

"Clear!" Ben hollered suddenly, slamming both fists down on the chest of the nearest mannequin.

Traci looked at him askance.

"I always wanted to do that," he explained, grinning sheepishly. "It looks so cool on TV."

"They don't use their fists," Traci said. "They have defibrillation paddles."

Ben nodded. "I know." Making his hands into two flat boards, he placed them carefully on the dummy. "Clear!" he bellowed again.

11

Jenna closed her eyes and concentrated on slow, even breathing. *Pace yourself*, she advised. *At this rate, certification is a long way off.*

"There you are. How was CPR training?" Mrs. Rosenthal asked, looking up from a magazine as Leah walked in through the front door of her family's condominium.

"Long," Leah answered. "And incredibly hot."

Her dad sat beside her mom on the sofa. "I thought you were going swimming afterwards," he said, taking in Leah's dusty shorts and dry hair. "What happened with that?"

"Miguel was busy."

Dropping her tote bag on the floor, Leah hurried into the kitchen before they could question her further. She was pretty annoyed with Miguel, actually, but she didn't want her parents to know that. They would be sure to take her side, which meant thinking bad things about him. No one was allowed to think bad things about Miguel but her.

I hate it when he gets this way, she sulked, choosing a bottled iced tea from the refrigerator and twisting off its cap. She had hoped to spend at least an hour or two alone with him that weekend, but the instant Traci had announced the end of that interminable CPR class, he had practically sprinted for his car, full of other plans.

"Where are you going?" Leah had asked, grabbing him by the back of his shirt. "I thought we were going swimming."

"What? Oh, I forgot. I can't," he'd said, his eyes still glued to the trailhead. "I've got stuff to do today, and besides, we'll get plenty of swimming in during water safety class."

"What kind of stuff?" she'd asked.

He'd waved a vague, impatient hand. "You know. Stuff."

If I knew, I wouldn't have asked, she thought, knocking back half of the sugary tea. It made her crazy when he shut her out, and now, with the clock ticking off the last few days of their senior year, she found it doubly insufferable.

"What about tomorrow, then?" she'd asked.

Miguel had scrunched up his face. "Mother's Day. I'm going to be busy with—"

"I know. Stuff," she had finished for him.

He hadn't even noticed her sarcasm.

She didn't want to be too hard on him. He definitely deserved some slack after the trauma he'd been through recently, when his favorite young patient at the hospital died. But still . . .

Being sad is no excuse for being rude. And anyway, today it was more like he was distracted or—

"Your dad and I want to talk about your birthday," Mrs. Rosenthal announced behind her, startling

Leah into nearly dropping her iced tea. She whirled around to see her parents standing at the kitchen counter, watching her curiously.

"You scared me," she complained.

Mr. Rosenthal ran his fingers through his hair, showing her his gray streaks. "If you think turning eighteen is scary, try forty."

"No thanks." Leah couldn't imagine being as old as her parents—and she wasn't eager to try.

"We thought you might like to have a party this year," Mrs. Rosenthal said.

Leah stifled a groan. Ever since she was in grade school, birthday fusses had embarrassed her. She liked the cake and presents, but she hated the teasing, the eyes turned her way, and the mandatory, self-conscious singing.

Oh, yeah. Especially the singing.

"Don't you think I'm a little old for that?" she asked hopefully.

"I'm not talking about Pin the Tail on the Donkey," her mother said wryly. "But this *is* your last birthday at home, and we want to make it special—especially since it's your eighteenth."

"How about inviting some of your friends over for dinner and cake?" her father suggested. "We could rent movies. Or, if we held it in the rec room downstairs, you kids could play pool, or even dance."

"I don't think we want to dance," Leah said quickly.

"Then don't," said her mom. "But it's only a week away now, so we need to invite people fast. Come on, Leah. What do you say?"

She wanted to say no, of course, but they were both looking at her so hopefully. And eighteen *was* a pretty big milestone. . . .

"I guess that might be fun," she allowed. "But only Eight Prime and maybe a few other people," she added. "I'll make the list. And no singing! I'll die if you make people sing that stupid song."

"What stupid song?" Mr. Rosenthal asked. "You don't mean 'Happy Birthday to You'?" The question launched him into spontaneous singing. "*Happy birthday to—*"

"Yes, *that* stupid song," said Leah, her cheeks hot at the mere idea. Maybe she wasn't too old for a party, but she was *way* too old for that. "I mean it, Dad. If you sing that in front of my friends, I'll have to pretend I don't know you."

Two

"No, Maggie! What are you doing?" Jenna snatched the can of whipped cream from her sister's hand before she could spray it into the bowl of strawberries Jenna was slicing. "You can't put that in there; it'll get all melty."

"Who made you the expert?" Maggie retorted, eyes snapping. Her damp auburn curls had been slicked down in preparation for church, but a few still corkscrewed in wild directions, as cantankerous as their owner. "If we mix the berries and whipped cream together, we can spoon it all onto the waffles at once. It'll be easier than doing it separate."

Caitlin turned away from the family's dual waffle irons. "No, Jenna's right, Maggie. I'll take care of the whipped cream. Why don't you go pour the juice?"

Maggie stuck out her tongue at Jenna as she grabbed a pitcher of orange juice off the counter, leaving to fill the glasses in the adjacent dining room.

"Are those sausages almost ready?" Caitlin asked.

"In a minute," Allison answered, pushing links around with a fork. "I like them real crispy outside."

Jenna peeked into the pan to make sure they weren't getting *too* crispy, then cut up her final strawberry and slipped a big piece to Sarah, who had been assigned the task of folding fancy napkins that Mother's Day morning, something she could do sitting on a barstool. Jenna was carrying the rest of the berries over to Caitlin when the telephone rang, startling everyone.

"I'll get it!" Sarah said eagerly, diving for the phone at the end of the breakfast bar.

"Who's calling *now*?" Jenna complained. Caitlin was just taking the platter of finished waffles out of the warming oven to add the final two. "Our breakfast is going to get cold!"

Every year the Conrad girls cooked breakfast as their Mother's Day gift—and so far this one actually looked edible. Not like the year they'd scorched the oatmeal, or that runny omelet disaster. Their mom always pretended that whatever they'd cooked was delicious, but Jenna had to eat it too, so she knew better. It would be horrible if this year—when delicious was finally a legitimate possibility—everything was ruined by one of those rude salespeople who called at mealtimes and wouldn't take no for an answer.

"Mary Beth!" Sarah squealed into the phone. "Hi! We're making breakfast!"

"Tell her we'll call back after we eat," Jenna said, waving to catch Sarah's attention. "We're ready to serve the food."

17

"These will keep a few more minutes," Caitlin said, putting all the waffles back into the oven.

"So will Mary Beth," Jenna insisted, but before she could argue further, Mrs. Conrad walked into the kitchen.

"Did I hear Mary Beth?" she asked Sarah, holding out her hand for the telephone.

Great timing, Jenna thought, annoyed. It was nice that her oldest sister had remembered Mother's Day, but couldn't she have remembered it *after* church? On the other hand, Mary Beth had been in charge the year of the oatmeal . . . and of the omelet . . .

Maybe she thinks she's doing Mom a favor.

"How are things in Nashville?" Mrs. Conrad was asking. "Don't you have finals next week?"

Jenna barely listened as she laid seven plates end to end on the counter, ready to fill them the second the call was over.

"Here, take that sausage out of the pan and drain it on this," she whispered to Allison, handing her an eighth plate lined with paper towels. "It's already crispy!" she insisted in response to Allison's dubious look.

Allison transferred the sausage, and Jenna threw more towels on top to soak up the grease. Then she took a pitcher of milk from the refrigerator and walked out to the dining table. Mr. Conrad was seated at its head, his nose buried in the Sunday paper.

"Hungry?" she asked as she poured milk into waiting glasses. Maggie had set down the orange juice pitcher halfway through the job and wandered off somewhere, she noticed.

"You bet," he answered, smiling over his paper. "What feast did you girls cook up this time?"

"You'll have to wait and see," she said mysteriously, although she was sure he already knew. The entire house smelled of waffles.

Jenna finished pouring the milk and then the juice, returning to the kitchen with two empty pitchers. Her mother was just hanging up the phone.

"That was Mary Beth," she announced, as if they didn't already know. "She's coming home again this summer!"

Caitlin had taken the waffles back out of the oven and was starting to put them on the plates. "Right when school gets out?" she asked. "Is she going to stay all summer?"

"She might show up a week or two late," their mother replied. "But yes, she's going to stay all summer. Isn't that terrific?"

Jenna grabbed Allison's plate of sausage and began dumping links next to waffles, barely aware of what she was doing. Mary Beth was going to be staying with them all summer? *Where* with them?

"I, uh—I really didn't think she'd come home again this year," Jenna ventured carefully; her mom had a hair trigger when it came to discussions of

19

living space. "I mean, she never said anything before, and she's so busy with her Nashville friends now. . . ."

"I know! Isn't it great?" Mrs. Conrad asked happily, tweaking Jenna's nose. "Just when you think it's over, we get her for one more year. This really *is* Mother's Day."

Jenna shot Caitlin a desperate look, but her sister only smiled as she sprayed blobs of whipped cream onto waffles.

But where is she going to stay? Jenna nearly shouted.

Was everyone just assuming she would move out of the third-floor room she shared with Caitlin and let Mary Beth have it back? Because that didn't seem fair at all—especially not now that she and Cat had grown so close. Jenna didn't want to room with anyone else.

Does Caitlin?

She took a deep breath. "I just think it's a lot to ask to have everyone switch their bedrooms around again just because—"

"What are you talking about?" her mother said. "Mary Beth will only be here a couple of months. She can sleep in Sarah's room."

"Goody!" cried Sarah, thrilled.

Mrs. Conrad smiled, and Jenna heaved a sigh of relief. Sarah was the only sister with her own bedroom, so if Mary Beth moved in with her, no one else would be disrupted. Jenna would get to stay with Caitlin.

She snuck another glance at her older sister, who had begun spooning up the strawberries with a dreamy, far-off smile, and knew instantly that she was thinking of David Altmann and the fact that he would soon be back in town as well. Once Caitlin's shyness had been like a wall between them; now Jenna could almost read her sister's mind.

Shy Caitlin wasn't hard to understand at all—a person just had to get to know her.

"Did you take the classifieds?" Melanie's father asked, digging through the Sunday paper. Still in his bathrobe at noon, he had pages spread all over the breakfast bar, completely oblivious to his unshaven cheeks, mussed brown hair, and the cheap reading glasses sliding down his thin nose.

"What would I do with the classifieds?" Melanie countered irritably, returning her attention to the open refrigerator. The Andrewses' part-time house-keeper, Mrs. Murphy, must have had more pressing things to do than go grocery shopping that week, judging by the lack of anything edible. There was half a loaf of bread, an expired tub of cottage cheese, and the usual surfeit of diet sodas and beer. Melanie found some American cheese in the meat drawer and was thinking of making a grilled cheese sandwich when her father looked up from his paper again.

"If you're going to make some toast, could you put in two slices for me?" he asked.

"I'm not making toast," she said sullenly.

"Oh. Could you put in two slices anyway?"

Melanie practically ripped two pieces of bread from the bag and stuffed them down into the toaster. Taking only a diet soda for herself, she slammed the refrigerator's stainless steel door, then stalked past her father and out of the kitchen.

"I'm going upstairs," she said over her shoulder. "You'll have to watch that bread yourself."

She thought she heard him grunt as she headed toward the stairs, but she didn't much care. If he ended up with burnt toast, that was his problem.

Does he even know it's Mother's Day? she wondered as her sneakers squeaked up the marble staircase. *He's reading the stupid newspaper. It must be in there somewhere.*

But if he knew, he hadn't given the least sign. Not one word. All he'd done was slob around in his bathrobe, get newsprint all over the bar, and ask her to make him toast.

Toast! When Mom was alive, we used to go to champagne brunch.

They had made a big deal of it every year, dressing up and driving to a fine restaurant in one of the classic cars her parents had collected. Melanie remembered it all as if it were yesterday: the smell of her mother's perfume, her father in a tie, the mouth-puckering sip of champagne she'd been allowed when the waiter wasn't looking. . . .

22

How could she be so nostalgic when her father didn't even know what day it was?

His memory must be as dead as the rest of him.

Which might not be such a bad thing, she reflected. But no matter how hard she tried to kill it off, her own memory was a voice inside her head, constantly bringing up things she didn't want to think about.

And it has so much to choose from.

Melanie pushed her bedroom door open, still lost in the past. At least she'd straightened out that mess with Steve Carson, her date for the prom and wannabe boyfriend. He had been upset when she'd told him it was over, but in the end his overly sensitive reaction had only made her more certain of her decision. She couldn't stand needy, clingy guys. Jesse had his faults, but at least he was never a wimp.

He was actually pretty nice to me yesterday, she thought, remembering Eight Prime's CPR class up at the lake. Although lately, when it came to her dealings with Jesse, she had to admit that she set her standard for "nice" pretty low. If no insults were exchanged, she called it a pretty good day.

I guess the same thing will go for Steve now too.

She had feared that facing him in art class for the rest of the semester would be some sort of nightmare, but she'd already survived the first two days, so she supposed she could last a couple more weeks. As long as he stayed mad enough not to speak to her, everything ought to be fine.

23

Walking across her plush carpet, Melanie stared out a window at the front of the Andrewses' large property. The sun was brilliant overhead, and the trees and grass had reached their peak of spring green. The clouds on the horizon seemed as puffy and harmless as white cotton candy.

It would be a good day to break out the lounge chairs, she thought idly. The swimming pool had been cleaned by the service the day before. The tiles were shiny, the water sparkling. . . .

But she just didn't feel like it. Her father was down there, for one thing, and she wasn't in the mood to talk to him again so soon.

She wasn't in the mood for much.

Sitting at her desk, she opened the bottom drawer and moved a stack of papers aside to reveal her mother's high school diary. She glanced back at her open bedroom door to make sure she was still unobserved, then lifted the leather-bound book out of hiding. The strap she had cut to defeat the lock dangled, and she was just about to open the covers when another of her mother's books caught her eye: a Bible. Melanie had found the Bible even before the diary, stuffed away at the back of a flat file in her mother's art studio. Its crinkly white leather cover and gilt-edged pages still looked as intimidating as ever, but Melanie found herself putting the diary down to pick up the Bible instead.

I was going to read this, she thought, letting the book fall open in her hands, *and I never got past all those begats.*

She lowered her nose to its pages and breathed in their odd yet familiar smell. Had the book smelled the same when her mother owned it? Or had age turned the paper more fragrant? Tucking the diary back into her desk, Melanie carried the Bible across the room, shutting her door before settling onto her bed.

Maybe I should have taken Peter's advice and tried reading a newer translation, she thought, flipping idly. *Or I could still skip to the New Testament, like he suggested, and see if that's any easier.*

Checking the table of contents, she learned that Matthew was the first book of the New Testament and turned to the appropriate page.

"This will be better," she told herself, snuggling into a pile of pillows, but a moment later she groaned. "*More* begats?"

At least there were fewer of them here. She began slogging though another ancient genealogy, hoping things would clear up as she went along.

Or I could always give in and borrow that study Bible Peter offered to lend me.

Melanie had been determined to read her mother's copy of the Bible, the book Tristyn had touched with her own hands, but a lot of time had passed since she had first tried, and she was starting to feel more practical. She struggled through a few more verses, then tossed the book aside in frustration.

That's it, she thought, giving up. *If this thing comes with Cliffs Notes, somebody bring them on.*

"You should have the lobster," Mr. Brewster urged his wife. "Treat yourself, for once."

"I don't know, Jimmy. It's so expensive," she said longingly.

"You deserve it. Come on! It's your day." He leaned closer, pointing to something on her menu. "Or how about the surf and turf? Steak *and* lobster."

"I couldn't possibly eat that much," Mrs. Brewster said with a little girl's pout. "You just want to see me get huge."

"I'll still love you when you do," he said, a rare twinkle in his eyes.

On the opposite side of the booth, Nicole rolled hers, praying no one from school was witnessing such a nauseating scene. Mother's Day gave her an ironclad excuse for appearing in public with her parents, but her folks seemed to think it was Valentine's Day instead. Nicole couldn't remember the last time she'd seen them act so mushy anywhere, let alone in a restaurant. It was abnormal. It was sickening. Most of all, it was completely embarrassing.

What's Dad so into this holiday for anyway? she wondered, averting her eyes and gazing out over the main dining room. *She's not his mother.*

The waiter finally came, and Mr. Brewster ordered lobster for his wife and chicken for himself. Heather had chicken too, and Nicole ordered a shrimp salad.

"Is salad going to be enough?" her father asked worriedly.

"It's pretty big," the waiter reassured him.

"Yeah, it's big," Nicole echoed as if she'd seen one, simultaneously vowing not to eat it all. Now that she'd been measured for her cheerleading uniform, she couldn't afford to gain an ounce. On the other hand, if she lost a pound or two . . .

I'll just have that much more room to move, she thought, picturing herself finishing off a perfect cheer with a series of flawless straddle jumps. No one could do that jump like Melanie, but maybe, if she practiced really hard . . .

The waiter walked away.

"Give Mom her present now," Heather whispered, elbowing Nicole in the ribs. The blow felt like a jackhammer on bones Nicole had worked hard to keep stripped of their padding.

"Knock it off," she whispered back, stiff-arming her sister to the opposite end of the booth.

"What are you girls doing?" Mrs. Brewster asked, the edge off her lovey-dovey expression.

"Nothing," Nicole said quickly. Digging into her purse, she slid a small gift-wrapped box across the table. "Here, I got you a present."

"*We* got you a present!" Heather said, delivering another elbow.

They jostled for better positions on the bench while their mother opened her gift.

"Oh, girls!" she exclaimed, lifting out a pair of pearl stud earrings. "How lovely!"

Nicole leaned back in the booth, vindicated. Heather had wanted to buy some stupid book, but Nicole had put her foot down.

"Mom will only read a book once, if that," she had argued. "She can wear earrings all the time."

Besides, considering that they were genuine pearls, they'd been an incredibly good deal. She and Heather were sure to get credit for spending more than they actually had.

Mr. Brewster held a pearl up to one of his wife's ears. "You look gorgeous," he said, in the same syrupy tone he'd been using all night. "The prettiest woman in the room."

"Oh, Jimmy," she giggled, practically batting her eyes in return.

Nicole felt her lip curl the way it always did right before she threw up.

"Put them on, Mom," Heather begged.

"The second we get home," Mrs. Brewster promised. "I don't think it would look nice to do that at the table."

Heather whined like a spoiled child while Nicole scanned the dining room again, making sure she was still unobserved by anyone who mattered. Now that she was a cheerleader, she couldn't be too careful who she was seen with.

And if I had to make a list of desirable associates, Heather would be the last person on it. Nicole pursed her lips, reconsidering. *All right, maybe second to last. Ben Pipkin gives her a pretty good run for the money.*

"Dad, can I have a Shirley Temple?" Heather broke off whining to ask abruptly.

"Sure."

Before anyone could stop her, Heather's arm snaked into the aisle, snagging a passing waiter by the back of his shirt and nearly upsetting his full food tray.

"Excuse me, can I have a Shirley Temple?" she asked in a voice pitched to be heard at a wrestling match. Heads turned at nearby tables. "You know that fizzy pink drink? With the cherries on top?"

The waiter nodded. "I'll see what I can do."

"Heather! You can't just grab people," Nicole scolded as the poor man made his escape. "That's not even our waiter!"

Heather stared as if Nicole had gone crazy. "What are you talking about? Of *course* that's a waiter."

"Mommm . . . ," Nicole began, hoping for some backup.

But her parents were whispering to each other and giggling again, acting like kids in the throes of puppy love.

Nicole squeezed her eyes shut and sank lower in the booth, wishing she were invisible. It wasn't that she didn't *like* her family . . .

She just liked them better when they all stayed home.

Three

"So, there it is," Miguel concluded, barely controlling the excitement in his voice. "If I can figure out how to get the down payment, this could actually work."

He and Leah had snagged a choice corner booth in Burger City during their lunch break that Monday, and she had initially been thrilled. But from the moment they'd ordered until her last sip of Coke, the only thing he'd talked about was some crazy scheme to buy Charlie Johnson's house. He had talked so much, in fact, that his fries had gotten cold. He hadn't even finished his hamburger.

"What do you think?" he prompted eagerly. "Wouldn't that be great?"

Leah worked to keep the scowl off her face. Despite the fact that Miguel and Jesse had recently painted its exterior, Charlie's claptrap old house still needed years of work. Worse, the neighborhood it was in, right next to public housing, was the most run-down in Clearwater Crossing. She could just imagine Miguel putting so much time into fixing the place that he'd forget she even existed. And even if he succeeded in making it a showpiece, then what? He'd have a rosebush in a wasteland, a jewel set in tin. In other words, not much.

"It's an interesting idea," she began carefully. "I just think—"

"The whole key is Charlie carrying the paper. I had no idea what he meant when he said he'd be willing to do that, but once I found out, I knew I was on to something."

Miguel had already explained that by carrying paper Charlie would be acting as his own bank, collecting monthly payments on the house plus earning interest. In effect, Charlie was lending the money a buyer would otherwise have to borrow somewhere else. Leah had never heard of such an arrangement; she wasn't even sure it sounded legal.

"Does your mom think this is a good idea?" she asked, wondering if Mrs. del Rios had any idea what her son was up to.

He flinched a little, and she knew she'd found the weak spot in his plan.

"There's no point telling her until I have the whole thing figured out," he said. "How to get the down payment, I mean. Why get her hopes up for nothing?"

"So you're sure she'll be excited about *that* house." Leah tried not to put too much emphasis on "that," but it came out stressed anyway.

"Of course! Why not?" Miguel gestured so wildly that he almost knocked over the catsup. "My family in a house of its own again, Leah—think of it! No bank is going to look at us now, not after my dad's bankruptcy. But with Charlie carrying paper . . . The house itself isn't nearly as important as getting back on our feet. Besides, I can always fix whatever's broken."

Leah smiled weakly. *Exactly what I was afraid of*.

"It'll be a lot of work for you," she said tentatively. "And you're going to be pretty busy already, with college and everything. I thought you and your mom were saving for a three-bedroom apartment."

"Charlie's house has three *bathrooms*," Miguel said, an acquisitive gleam in his eyes. "Four bedrooms and an office, plus that big living room and kitchen. Can you imagine how cool? We'd have entire rooms with nothing in them."

"Do you *need* empty rooms? I mean, our condo's not that big and my family gets along fine."

"You think it's a bad idea," he said.

"I didn't say that. I just—"

"Good. Because I'm going to do it. If there's any way at all . . ."

A large group of students headed for the door, prompting Miguel to check his watch. "Oops. We'd better get out of here," he said, stuffing cold fries into his mouth.

"We don't want to be late," Leah agreed, relieved

to be off the hook about Charlie's. "If we start getting demerits now, they might not let us attend the senior picnic or grad night trip."

She was kidding, of course. As squeaky clean as their records were, there was no way they could suddenly rack up enough demerits to keep them out of graduation activities. Even so, she didn't much like the way Miguel shrugged as he pushed the restaurant door open.

"Who cares about all that stupid high school stuff?" he asked scornfully. "I've got bigger fish to fry."

Nicole sat ramrod straight on her favorite bench in the CCHS quad, concentrating on keeping her shoulders back and her gut sucked in. Now that she was a cheerleader, she was on display every moment of every day, and she intended to pass random inspections. Of course, her appearance would be even more important when the rest of the school found out that she'd been put on the cheerleading squad, but she was dressed her best that Monday anyway, not taking any chances.

It would be nice if Sandra had made some sort of official announcement. Or at least put a sign up on the gym, the way she did with the first list, Nicole thought, wondering how many of the passing students were actually aware of her change in status. It didn't much matter, though. Any news as important as a substitution on the cheerleading squad was sure to get around pretty fast.

"I wish you would stop reading," Nicole told Courtney Bell abruptly. "I might as well be sitting here by myself."

Courtney looked up from her book, pushing red curls out of her eyes. "What do you want?"

"What do you mean, what do I want?" Nicole returned, annoyed. "I want you to talk to me. What are you studying for, anyway? Finals aren't until next week."

"This isn't for school." Courtney made a face. "Are you kidding? During lunch? No, I got this out of the library."

She held up the book in her lap, turning its cover toward Nicole.

"*Transcendent Personal Power,*" Nicole read aloud. "What is that about?"

"Oh, you have to read it! It's the coolest book. Full of all these things I've been thinking but didn't know how to say."

"Like what?"

"Listen to this." Courtney flipped to a page she had marked. " 'When we empower ourselves, we teach others to empower us. Power is breath, flowing in and out of our bodies; most people lose it the instant they perceive it. But power can reside in us if we build containers of peace and purpose. Quieting our minds, we call power to ourselves. We are strongest in our silence.'" Courtney looked up, a half-awed smile on her face. "Isn't that *cool?*" she demanded.

Nicole could feel her own blank look. "I guess so. What does it mean?"

Courtney's jaw dropped. "What do you mean, what does it mean? Weren't you listening?"

"I thought I was. But . . . well . . . what I heard didn't make much sense."

"It's all about *power,*" Courtney explained impatiently. "*Personal* power. You know?"

"Oh. You mean like *transcendent* personal power."

"Exactly!" Courtney exclaimed, not catching the irony. She returned to her reading, and Nicole gazed off across the quad, confused.

Ever since Kyle Snowden had dumped her at the prom, Courtney hadn't been herself. Not that the change was entirely bad. She was taking fewer shots at people, and that part was definitely good. Nicole felt like she could breathe again without constantly anticipating the next sarcasm. But if Courtney was less antagonistic, perhaps it was partly because she was paying less attention. She seemed completely wrapped up in herself these days, bent on some new agenda. The old Courtney wouldn't have been caught dead reading self-help books—much less taking them seriously.

And is it just me, or is that particular book really stupid? The part she just read sounded more like gibberish and double-talk than useful advice. How can Courtney think it means anything at all?

Nicole glanced over to see Courtney totally absorbed in reading again, a half-eaten chocolate bar melting on top of a flattened lunch bag beside her. That sight alone was worth a thousand words—her best friend had definitely changed.

"Hi, Nicole," a male voice said suddenly.

Nicole snapped to attention just in time to make eye contact with a guy who was walking by.

"Hi, uh, Noel," she said, her heart up in her throat.

Noel Phillips was a totally cute junior who everyone said would be senior class president next year. Not quite as good as quarterback, maybe, but still . . . a big step up for her. Especially since he had never noticed her before. She hadn't even known he knew her name.

The second Noel was out of hearing, Nicole spun around to face Courtney. "What do you think of that?" she asked triumphantly.

Courtney looked wearily up from her book. "What now?"

"Don't tell me you didn't see that! Noel Phillips just said hello to me!"

"Really?" Courtney's eyes flicked listlessly over the crowd. "Where is he?"

"He's gone *now*, Court. I can't believe you missed it. He was totally smiling at me and everything."

Courtney shrugged slightly. "I wouldn't have thought he was your type."

"You're missing the whole point! Noel Phillips knows who I am. Word must be starting to spread about me making cheerleader." Nicole was so excited that she could barely contain herself.

But Courtney only nodded. "Oh," she said, returning to her book.

She's hopeless today! thought Nicole, suppressing an urge to push her friend off the bench. How was she supposed to relish her big moment if no one enjoyed it with her? *I mean, it's great that she's Ms. Peace and Love and all, but does she have to be Space Girl too?*

"Um, hi, Steve," Melanie murmured, clutching her books to her chest.

His icy stare held her gaze a moment before he looked pointedly in the other direction, his lips a hard, straight line.

Okay, fine. So this is the game we're playing. Melanie hurried past him in the row and took her seat in the back of art class. *The only reason I said hello to him in the first place was because he was looking right at me.*

Even so, it was embarrassing to have him treat her that way, and her face was hot as she wondered who had noticed. Luckily, most of her art class seemed to be trickling in late that afternoon.

From now on, I'll be late too, she decided. *I'll wait until just before the tardy bell, then walk around the edge*

*of the room and come up to my seat from behind. Steve
and I never need to make eye contact again.*

It was a stupid, juvenile plan, she knew. It was the
only plan she had.

I can't wait for summer vacation to end all this drama,
she thought, leaning back in her seat as Mr. McIntosh entered the room.

Luckily, they were working in pencil and charcoal
for the last two weeks of class, which meant there
was no need to wander around collecting supplies.
Melanie took out her sketch pad and flipped it open
even before Mr. McIntosh began setting up the objects to be drawn: a series of glass and metal vases.

*Going out with Steve was the biggest mistake I ever
made,* she thought, beginning to sketch almost without seeing. *If I hadn't gone to the prom with him, I could
have gone with Jesse.*

Her pencil scratched back and forth on the paper,
but her mind was far away.

*Maybe I could catch Jesse after class. I could make an
excuse to walk past his locker, then pretend seeing him
there was an accident.*

She had never done anything like that before, so
maybe he would buy it.

Except what would I say? She tried to picture the
encounter. *Hi, Jesse. I was just in the neighborhood, so I
thought I'd stop by and ask if there's any chance that you
might want me back.*

Oh, yeah. That'll happen.

Melanie sighed and began to pay a little more attention to her work. The outlines of her vases took shape quickly, but it was harder getting the shading right. She kept filling in, then erasing, filling in, then erasing, trying to create the transparency of glass and the luster of metal. Eventually she was satisfied, and by the time the bell finally rang she had already packed up her things, itching to be on her way.

Hurry, she thought, pushing out the door into the rapidly filling hallway. *Get there before he leaves.*

She reached Jesse's locker just as he was slamming its door, catching him in the nick of time.

"Hi, Jesse. What are you doing?" She'd meant to sound casual, but her voice brayed out, betraying her nervousness. She winced and hoped he hadn't noticed.

He turned around with a book in his hands. "Going to class. How about you?"

"Yes. I mean . . . obviously."

He gave her a tentative smile. She smiled back. He shook his head a little, as if uncertain what they were doing, then shrugged and walked away.

Brilliant! she groaned silently, slumping against the nearest wall. *Oh, that went well. What was I thinking?*

She couldn't claim to have any idea.

On the other hand, he did smile at me.

Maybe all wasn't lost. Melanie closed her eyes, recapturing that grin, envisioning his long brown bangs pushed off to one side and the puzzled expression in his blue eyes. . . .

He looked cute in that rugby shirt. I wonder——

The first bell rang, startling her back to the present. The tardy bell would follow in two minutes.

Great, she thought, beginning the sprint to her last class. How could she have lost track of the time that way, in the middle of the main hall? She had practically forgotten she was at school.

Maybe because school seems so pointless this late in the year. Except for a few last projects and finals, there wasn't anything left to do. She felt like she was just going through the motions, putting in an appearance. Half the time her brain wasn't even engaged.

All you have to do is keep it together for two more weeks, Andrews, she told herself as she ran. *Do you think you can handle that?*

Four

"So when is David's graduation?" Jenna asked at lunchtime on Tuesday. She followed up her question with a bite of salami sandwich.

Peter put down his juice. "We're leaving Thursday after school. He graduates Friday, and we'll be back on Saturday in time for water safety class. You *are* going to help Chris with the Junior Explorers this weekend, right? Because I won't be back that early."

"I already talked to Maura," Jenna assured him, naming Chris Hobart's longtime girlfriend. "All three of us will be there."

"Good. The kids won't miss me, then."

"No. But you'll miss them," Jenna said, smiling.

Ever since Peter and Chris had begun the Junior Explorers program to provide some fun for disadvantaged kids, Peter had devoted himself heart and soul to the cause. The smile on Jenna's face grew as she realized once again how lucky she was to have him for a boyfriend.

"So is David coming home with you Saturday?" she asked.

"Yep. We're going to help him get packed after the ceremony. Hopefully between the car he just bought and ours we can figure out how to bring all his stuff home."

"You ought to take the Junior Explorers' bus."

Peter laughed. "Can't you just see us driving up in that? David got his commercial license, though, so he's going to be able to drive the kids."

"This is all working out perfectly!" Jenna said happily.

When Chris said he didn't have enough free time to help run a summer day camp, it had originally looked like a pretty big problem. Not only did the camp bus driver have to be at least eighteen, but the park service also expected them to have full-time adult supervision as well as a trained lifeguard. The situation had looked dire, until Peter's older brother had saved the day by volunteering to serve as camp director. David had said he needed a break after college, and that volunteering at camp would still leave him plenty of time to polish his résumé and start sending it around. Personally, Jenna suspected he had another, more romantic, reason as well.

"Caitlin's really excited about David coming home," she said. "She thinks I don't know it, but the two of them have been sending e-mails back and forth like crazy."

"They do seem pretty serious."

"Maybe we'll all have a double wedding someday," Jenna blurted without thinking.

Peter grinned. "Don't I have to ask you to marry me first?"

I can't believe I said that! she thought, mortified. She looked down at their blue plastic table, then shifted her gaze out across the quad, up to the puffy clouds sweeping the southern sky, over to the main building—anywhere but at Peter.

"So, did you think of a name for the camp yet?" she asked to change the subject.

" 'Camp Clearwater' is my best idea so far. I'm still open to something catchier, but—"

" 'Camp Clearwater' is nice," Jenna said quickly. "No one will have any trouble remembering that. Did you send out those registration forms you were talking about?"

"Yep. I mailed them out to the kids' parents last night, along with that tentative activities schedule." Peter crossed his fingers. "I hope we get a good response."

"For a free day camp? Are you kidding? The Explorers will probably bring all their friends."

"That would be fine with me. The more, the merrier."

The bell rang, putting an end to Jenna's lingering embarrassment.

"All we have to do now is get Eight Prime certified in water safety," he added as the two of them rose from the table. "That's the last big hurdle."

Jenna frowned and pulled her backpack onto her

shoulders. "I hope people are going to take that class more seriously than they did first aid and CPR. If there had been any more fooling around during CPR, I might have strangled someone."

Peter laughed. "We passed."

"I'm not kidding!" she insisted. "One more story from Ben or sarcastic comment from Jesse could have pushed me right over the edge."

"Oh, sure. Blame it on the guys," Peter teased. "You didn't notice Nicole checking her makeup every five minutes?"

She had, actually. And Melanie sketching who knew what in the dirt with a stick. And Leah hanging on Miguel.

"People had better get serious. That's all I'm saying. Because if they don't, I'll have to take charge."

"How exactly do you plan to do that?" he asked, still laughing.

She had no idea, but instead of admitting it, she put on a mock-tough expression. "Just hope you don't have to find out."

"Sandra! Hi!" Melanie called, running the last few steps to meet up with the cheerleading coach. School had let out only minutes before, and Sandra was striding along against the foot traffic on CCHS's front lawn.

"What are you doing here now?" Melanie asked. "Is the squad having a meeting today?"

"Tomorrow," Sandra said coolly, barely glancing Melanie's way. Her neck seemed stiffer than the starch in her collar, and she didn't slow her steps a bit. If anything, she sped up.

Melanie had to reverse direction to stay at the coach's side. "Oh," she said, sensing a chill. "I just thought, since you're here—"

"I have some paperwork."

"Oh," Melanie repeated, feeling suddenly foolish. She didn't even know why she was still following, except that she and Sandra had always been friendly in the past. And Melanie *had* been hoping to ask her something. . . .

"So you got Nicole added to the squad with no problem?" Melanie ventured, even though it wasn't what she had really wanted to ask. She already knew the answer, for one thing, but it would never do if Sandra found out that Melanie and Nicole were in collusion. Sandra took cheerleading seriously; she was certain to be furious if Melanie's real reason for dropping off the squad ever came to light.

A nod was Sandra's only acknowledgment.

"You guys are all set, then. Right? I mean, my leaving didn't cause any problems."

Sandra remained silent.

"Right?" Melanie repeated, a little desperately.

"You don't need to worry about us anymore, Melanie. You wanted out, and you're out. I'll take things from here."

"It's not that I wanted out so much as—"

Sandra gave her a sharp look.

"I mean . . . there were some things." Melanie tried to cover lamely. "But next year, who knows? Stuff changes. So if you were to get an opening in the fall . . ."

Sandra stopped in her tracks. "I really don't see that happening," she said bluntly. "You made your decision, Melanie. Now, if you don't mind, I need to get some work done."

"Right. Um, okay," Melanie stammered, stunned, as her coach walked off. She hadn't expected Sandra to be *happy* with her for dropping out, but she hadn't expected her to be so angry, either. After all, the school still had a good squad; the only person Melanie had hurt was herself.

Not even me. Not really.

Although she had to admit she was sorry now to be missing cheerleading camp. And Tanya and Angela had both made her feel like a criminal for leaving the squad, even though she hadn't told them the real reason why. Every time the topic came up, she just said she was tired of school, claimed to have a lot of other things to do, and quickly changed the subject.

Still, every time the topic came up, she regretted her decision more.

Dropping off the squad was entirely your own idea, she reminded herself. *No one made you do it.*

And it *had* given Nicole the thrill of all time.

Melanie watched as her former coach disappeared

47

into the main building. *So I'm not a cheerleader anymore. And it looks like I may never be one again.*

She shrugged. *I'll survive. I always do.*

Leah was walking the last block to her condominium building when somebody called her name from the other side of the street. She turned to see a sporty blue car parked at the curb, the guy behind the wheel grinning like the Cheshire Cat.

"Shane!" she exclaimed.

He climbed out of the car and jogged over to meet her.

"What are you doing here? Again," she added pointedly.

The last—and only other—time Shane Garrett had appeared at her home had also been unexpected. He had claimed then that he needed to drop off a late paper for a class he was taking from her father. Leah hadn't been sure she believed his excuse, but she was positive she'd made it clear he shouldn't try that again. Her father wasn't big on students who missed deadlines.

"Assuming my dad is even home, you really don't want to disturb him," she began, before Shane had even stopped walking. "You'll be much better off if you—"

"Relax," Shane interrupted. "He *is* home, and if I wanted to disturb him, I'd have followed him in when I saw him drive up. I came here to see you."

He closed the last few steps, flashing her another of the flirty smiles she had come to recognize as his trademark. His wavy black hair was combed straight back, and beneath the hem of his faded shorts, his legs were hard with the type of muscle rarely seen on high school guys. The sight made her even more aware of the age difference between them.

"Me?" she said weakly. "What for?"

Shane rolled his eyes. "You're not really that innocent. Are you?"

The question made her squirm. Ever since she'd met Shane at a picnic on the Clearwater University campus, he'd been pretty open about his interest in her. She should have told him about Miguel immediately; she still wasn't sure how that subject had gotten skipped. But since she had somehow omitted mentioning her relationship then, it was definitely time to do it now. Shane would have to back off once he knew she was already taken.

"I have a boyfriend," she blurted out. "His name's Miguel, and I would have said something sooner, but I kind of thought you knew. Then, by the time I figured out you didn't—"

"I do."

"What?"

"I do know. Your father mentioned how engrossed you are with the guy, which I don't think he likes much, by the way. Why else would he have introduced you to me?"

49

"You—I—you're kidding," Leah stammered. "My father *likes* Miguel."

Shane shrugged. "Okay. But it's a big world out there, Leah. Maybe he just thinks you ought to see more of it before you let someone tie you down."

"I am not tied down!" she protested.

"Oh, good," he said, a mischievous glint in his eyes. "Can we go get a pizza, then? I'm starving."

"Now?"

"Why not now?"

"Well, for one thing, it's barely four o'clock."

Shane threw back his head and laughed, a perfect display of white teeth and deep dimples. "If that's your biggest objection, I am so in."

"Well, it's not. It's *not* my biggest objection," she said quickly. Her heart was thundering, and there was a weak, empty feeling in the pit of her stomach. "If you had asked me as a friend, then maybe I could have gone. But now, after what you just said . . ." Leah shook her head. "Miguel is my boyfriend, tried and true."

"Fine. I understand," said Shane, flipping one wrist as if tired of the discussion. "But that's no reason you and I can't be friends, is it? In a few months, we'll both be at Stanford. And, according to your father, Miguel will still be right here. Is he even going to college?"

"Of course. He's going to CU," she said defensively, choosing to ignore the fact that he still hadn't received an acceptance.

He will, though, she thought loyally. Besides, there was no way she was going to let the love of her life look bad in front of Shane I'm-So-Irresistible Garrett.

I don't even like the guy.

Much.

She and Miguel were far too committed for her to ever be swayed just by Shane's good looks. Or that cute bad-boy sparkle in his brown eyes. Or even by how smart he was, or how fun he could be to talk to—when the subject was more to her liking.

Shane's gaze was still on her face. She had the sudden uneasy feeling he was reading her mind.

"So are we going for pizza or what?" he asked.

"You're impossible!" she cried.

He shook his head. "Not really. I'm partial to pepperoni, but I'll eat anything but anchovies. You don't like anchovies, do you? Good," he said, not waiting for her answer, "because that would ruin everything."

"Really? I *love* anchovies," she lied.

"Two-second rule," he laughed. "The first reaction is always the real one. Nice try, though. You might have fooled Miguel."

"How do you know? You don't even know Miguel."

The mischievous smile was back on his lips. "And that makes everything possible."

51

Five

"Wish me luck," Nicole said as she and Courtney approached the open classroom door.
Inside, the new cheerleading squad was about to
hold its lunchtime meeting—Nicole's first.

Courtney brushed off her friend's request. "You
don't need it. What for?"

The girls stopped in the hallway and Nicole
peeked around the doorjamb far enough to see most
of the rest of the squad. Sandra wasn't there yet, and
it seemed kind of awkward to walk in and join the
group without the coach to introduce her.

"Do I look all right?" she asked Courtney nervously.

"You look fine. Like you scored a first date with
the guy of your dreams," Courtney added, a trace of
the old sarcasm back in her voice.

Is she saying I'm overdressed?

Nicole had spent hours the night before agonizing
over her hair and clothes, and she'd gotten up extra
early that Wednesday morning to do her very best

52

makeup. She poked her head around the doorway again, to check on what the other girls were wearing.

Well, maybe I went a little overboard. But not much. Besides, this is like a first date. I need to make a good impression!

"You're going to the library, right?" Nicole asked. "If I get out early, I'll come find you."

"You won't get out early," Courtney predicted. "Besides, if I find the book I want, I'll probably take it out on the grass somewhere."

Whatever, thought Nicole, shaking her head.

Courtney had hardly stopped reading lately, as if having her nose in a book was her latest fashion statement. At least today Nicole wouldn't have to sit and watch while Courtney gleaned more pearls of self-help wisdom from her guru du jour. More importantly, she wouldn't have to pretend to appreciate any of the garbage that Court read aloud.

Nicole spotted Sandra coming down the hallway. "Okay, I'm going in now," she said. "See you later."

She scuttled into the classroom before Courtney could reply, in a hurry to make her entrance. Nicole wanted Sandra to be there, but she didn't want the other girls to think she was joined to the coach's hip.

The rest of the squad had already pulled chairs into three clusters. Returning cheerleaders Tanya Jeffries, Lou Anne Simmons, and Angela Maldonado were clearly the premier group—but did Nicole dare to try to join them? She had the advantage of knowing Tanya and Angela from the times they'd helped out with Eight Prime projects, but she didn't want them to think she was presuming on that minor past acquaintance. On the other hand, if they accepted her into their circle . . .

"Hi, Tanya," Nicole ventured, sidling up to the new team captain. Tanya and Melanie had originally been named cocaptains, but with Melanie gone Tanya had the honor all to herself.

"Hello," Tanya said coolly.

Angela glanced at her and then quickly away.

Lou Anne didn't even look up from the cheerleading camp brochure she was reading.

Was it Nicole's imagination, or were they not too happy to see her?

She glanced nervously from Tanya's group to the four girls sitting in the next circle. She recognized Debbie Morris, the junior who had been so superior about making the squad when Nicole was only runner-up. Debbie was sitting with Sidney Wallace, Maria Martinez, and . . .

Nicole was still trying to put a name to the fourth girl when Sandra walked into the room.

"Okay, let's get these chairs into one big circle," Sandra said, sparing Nicole the embarrassment of having to crash somebody's group. "And be quick because we don't have much time today."

Nicole rushed to grab a chair and drag it into the circle before it could close, not caring who she ended up next to as long as she was part of the group. Even moving quickly, though, she practically had to force her way in, tangling her chair's metal legs with Debbie's chair on one side and Kara Tibbs's on the other.

"Oops. Sorry," Nicole muttered, trying to wrestle her chair free. There had been a gap there when she'd started, but now the space was so tight that she couldn't pull her chair away from Debbie's without getting more tangled up in Kara's. For a second, clanging filled the room, drowning out everything else. Debbie held her position, not giving an inch, as Nicole's cheeks heated up. Finally Kara pulled her chair back a bit. Nicole centered hers in the still-tight space and flashed Kara a quick, grateful smile, not even caring that the mousy-haired sophomore was the least popular girl on the squad.

"If we could all just settle down . . . ," Sandra said, a little testily.

Nicole dropped to her seat, the chair incident already forgotten.

This is my squad, she thought proudly, looking around the circle at her fellow cheerleaders' faces. *These are the girls I'll go to cheerleading camp with, and hang out with all next year. We're going to be like sisters! The good kind of sisters*, she added immediately. *Not like me and Heather.*

"First off," Sandra said, taking her seat at the top of the circle, "did everyone meet Nicole? As I'm sure you've all heard by now, Melanie decided to leave the squad, and Nicole is taking her place. Please welcome her aboard."

Sandra waved a hand in her direction and Nicole snapped to attention, beaming her biggest, brightest smile.

But nobody smiled back. Not really. There were a few halfhearted shrugs. Tanya and Angela nodded at her. But that was it. No one applauded. No one even said hello. Then, as quickly as the eyes had turned her way they were gone, fixed on their coach again.

Oh, my God, they hate me! Nicole realized. *Nobody wants me here at all!*

"All right. Who has camp brochures?" Sandra asked. "Pass them all up to me."

Brochures started making their way to Sandra, but Nicole was so shaken that she barely noticed the leaflets passing through her fingers. Her eyes were focused on all the faces not looking in her direction.

What did I do wrong? she wondered desperately. Surely this couldn't be about tangling up a chair. *Although I guess that didn't make me look very graceful. Maybe they think I won't be able to cut it.*

After all, she had been Sandra's last choice, while Melanie had been one of Sandra's two first.

Maybe that's what the problem is. They're mad at me because they'd rather have Melanie.

If they were, it wasn't fair. It wasn't her fault Melanie had dropped out.

Well, maybe it was. But they don't know that.

"Okay, do I have all the brochures now?" Sandra selected one and held it up. "What did everyone think of Camp Twist-n-Shout?"

"That one looks good," Tanya said. "I like the way you do more things with only your squad and not the entire camp."

"I *want* to do things with the whole camp," Lou Anne protested. "We have a whole year to keep to ourselves. I like that other one. No, the red one," she said, pointing to Sandra's pile.

"Except that at Twist-n-Shout, we could take a stunt clinic," Angela said.

"Why don't we just go to stunt camp?" Debbie asked. "We already know how to dance and cheer."

Nicole tried to follow the conversation, but she was so distraught that the words barely registered. Here she was, finally where she wanted to be, and she might as well have been invisible. No one talked to her, no one noticed her, no one even *looked* at her.

She didn't exist.

I'll win them over, she vowed, making sure her fake smile never left her lips. *I'll make them like me if it kills me.*

She hadn't come so far to give up now. Getting onto the cheerleading squad was the hardest thing she'd ever done, and if she had to work a little longer to make people accept her, it was a price she was willing to pay. Besides, it was still only May; the new squad wouldn't start performing until fall. Before that there was the rest of the current school year, plus cheerleading camp, plus the entire summer.

Not that it's going to take that long, Nicole promised herself, ratcheting up her smile another notch. *I'll just lie low awhile, kiss a few butts . . . and when we get to camp, I'll memorize every routine I see. I'll memorize when to breathe. Pretty soon I'll be so indispensable that they'll forget all about Melanie.*

Her smile turned more genuine at the thought.

By fall I'll have them eating from my hand.

"Are you sure you want to do this in a bikini?" Jenna asked Nicole. "I mean, things could get kind of physical." She tugged nervously at her old Speedo, making sure her back view was covered.

"This is a good suit on me," Nicole replied, running one hand down her board-flat stomach. "Besides, it's the only red one I have."

"I don't think our suits *have* to be red," said Jenna. *I hope not, anyway,* she added. Hers was navy blue, but it was the only suit she had dared to wear to Eight Prime's first water safety class that Wednesday afternoon. After all, at some point they were going to be pretending to rescue each other, weren't they? Dragging each other around, simulating CPR, maybe even carrying people up the beach—she really had no idea what the class might entail. She only knew she'd die if anything private peeked out.

"What's our instructor like?" Nicole asked, glancing from their spot on the dock back toward the cabin, where the rest of Eight Prime was taking turns changing.

Jenna shook her head. "I've never met him. But I hope he gets here soon."

"I hope he's cute."

Nicole kicked an acorn off the boards into the green water. Her toenails were red, to match her suit, and suddenly Jenna had something else to feel self-conscious about. Her own polish was weeks old, chipped down to tiny patches. She hadn't thought of it before; now she realized too late that everyone was going to be seeing her feet.

Everyone's going to be seeing more than that, she thought nervously, anxious about the group's first event in bathing suits. Not that she was ashamed of her body—exactly. She was simply happier with more clothes on.

"Here come Melanie and Leah," Nicole announced, looking toward the cabin.

The girls were walking barefoot across the packed-dirt clearing, towels slung over their shoulders, puffs of dust catching sunbeams wherever they stepped. Jenna heaved a sigh of relief that neither of their bathing suits was red. Melanie had on a two-piece flowered print, with a sports bra top and boy-short bottoms. Leah was wearing a green striped maillot similar to Jenna's.

"The guys are all in there changing now," Leah announced, walking onto the dock. "Has anyone seen our instructor?"

"I hope he's cute," said Melanie.

"Oops," said Leah. "I think you just got your wish."

Everyone looked toward the trailhead. A tall, lean blond had just emerged from the trees wearing nothing but flip-flops, a tan, and some low-slung red shorts. His sun-streaked hair was uncombed, framing his face like a messy halo. Similarly golden hair curled on his strong limbs and ran in a perfect line from his chest to his navel, which was underscored by a tribal tattoo.

"Wow," breathed Nicole.

"I saw him first," said Melanie.

"No, I did," Leah reminded them.

"You already have a boyfriend," the other two said in unison.

"So do you, Nicole," said Jenna. "What about Guy?"

Guy Vaughn was not only cute and nice, he was also one of the most talented singers Jenna had ever met. But Nicole screwed up her face like he gave her some kind of pain.

"Guy and I aren't married," she said. "Besides, Guy's not here."

Melanie's eyes were still fixed on their new instructor, who had begun ambling across the clearing toward them. "I wonder if anything's pierced," she mused, giving the impression that she'd like to explore that further.

"You guys aren't going to flirt with the instructor. Are you?" Jenna asked worriedly. "That's the only person who volunteered to teach us this class for free, and if we do anything to upset him—"

Melanie laughed and tossed her thick hair. "I may be out of practice, but don't worry. The guys *I* flirt with don't get upset."

Nicole pursed her lips slightly, an envious expression in her blue eyes. With an obvious effort, she shook it off. "*I'm* not going to flirt," she announced haughtily. "It wouldn't be fair to Guy."

"More for me," Melanie told her with a canary-eating grin.

Jenna's panic must have shown in her face, because a moment later Melanie shoved her playfully.

"I'm kidding! Come on. He's, like, twenty-five."

"Oh. Good."

But Jenna still wasn't entirely convinced. Even after all this time, some days she felt like she barely knew Melanie. Her pretty face gave away so little, and her eyes were so hard to read. . . .

"Are you all here for water safety?" their new

instructor asked, reaching them on the dock. "My name's Ken, and I'm supposed to meet some guy named Peter?"

"He'll be here any second," Jenna said quickly, not trusting the others—or at least two of the others—to speak. "In fact, here he comes now," she added, relieved to spot the guys trotting out to meet them.

She introduced the girls while they waited, determined to pay no attention to the fact that Ken was even cuter up close. *It's not like it matters*, she thought, irritated. *I wouldn't even have noticed if Melanie and Nicole hadn't put it into my head.*

"Hi. You must be Ken," Peter said, jogging onto the dock.

He was just stretching out his hand to shake when a loud, incredibly poor imitation of a Tarzan yell rang out. Everyone swiveled around to see Ben bearing down on them, his red swim trunks flapping like an unpacked parachute. Jenna stepped instinctively to the edge of the dock, clearing the center aisle just as Ben thundered past her on the boards, flinging himself off the end in a bent-legged maneuver somewhere between a dive and a belly flop. The amount of water that splashed up was phenomenal—completely out of proportion to Ben's bony frame. Nicole squealed indignantly as a cold wave caught her across the stomach.

"What are you doing? You—you, *stupid*!" she

yelled when his head popped up, drying her body with her bare hands. "Did anyone tell you to go in the water? I wasn't ready to get wet!"

"Sorry," Ben said meekly. "I was just having a little fun."

He started to paddle for the shore, then froze, looking toward the group on the dock with an expression of pure terror.

"Right. Safety lesson number one," Ken told him. "Never, *ever* dive off anything until you have checked the depth of the water. You could have been seriously hurt."

Ben didn't answer. Something told Jenna that a belated attack of safety consciousness wasn't his problem.

"What's the matter, Ben?" she asked. "Why don't you swim in?"

"I, uh, um . . ."

Jesse walked out to the very end of the dock and peered down into the water. "Lost your shorts," he announced. "Good one."

Ben started swimming again then—backward. "They're in here somewhere," he said, blushing purple as he flailed his limbs around in an underwater search. "I just have to find them."

Without warning, Miguel pushed Jesse in. "Give Ben a hand there," he said, laughing, as Jesse sputtered to the surface.

"No! No, I can do it myself!" The thrashing of Ben's legs made the top half of his body jerk like the shark-attack victims in *Jaws*.

Ignoring Ben, Jesse reached up and caught Miguel by an ankle, pulling him into the lake with a splash.

"Ha!" Miguel cried. "War!"

He and Jesse started dunking each other, Ben's swimsuit completely forgotten.

"Look over there, Ben," Leah said, pointing. "No. Over *there*. I think I see something red."

"Besides his face?" asked Melanie.

Jenna could feel her own cheeks flushing as Ken turned to her and Peter.

"Are you guys always this, uh . . . rambunctious?" he asked.

"No," she said, so embarrassed that she actually wished she could jump in and find Ben's shorts herself. At least the water would be cool.

"No. I'm really sorry," Peter said. "Ben is . . . Ben. But he means well. And we're all completely committed to passing this class."

"Unless it conflicts with one of my cheerleading meetings," Nicole butted in. "The squad is my first priority now." The smile she flashed Ken left Jenna wondering if she had forgotten her promise not to flirt.

"I'm going to help Ben find his suit," Jenna announced, preparing to jump off the dock.

"No girls!" Ben screamed. "No girls in the water!"

"I'll go," Peter said, stepping off in her place. He

disappeared with barely a splash, a flurry of bubbles closing over his head. When he surfaced he broke up Miguel's water fight, and soon all four guys were feeling along the lake bottom with their toes, trying to find Ben's trunks.

"If those things weren't big enough to fumigate a house, maybe they wouldn't have sunk," Jesse said. "The pockets are probably full of water."

"Rocks," Ben admitted. "I was going to skip them later."

"Brilliant!" said Nicole, rolling her eyes.

Jenna squeezed her own eyes shut for fear of meeting Ken's again.

Are we ever going to get certified? she worried. *Maybe, after we find his shorts, Ben should just watch from the dock.*

Certified or not, they definitely didn't want him in charge of saving anyone.

"Well. So. After we found Ben's shorts, that didn't go too badly," Melanie said to Jesse's back. The two of them had been the last to take Ken's official swimming test, and now they were the last ones left on the shore.

Jesse stopped toweling his hair and turned to face her, his wet brown locks standing out in all directions. Tiny rivulets ran down his body, traveling the bumps of his tan abdomen before disappearing into his suit and dripping from the hem of his shorts.

Melanie's heart squeezed at the sight, making her hope the other girls had bought her supposed interest in Ken. It might keep them from noticing who she was really pining for.

"We didn't *do* anything," he said. "Not anything we didn't already know."

Which was true. Ken hadn't taught them rescues that afternoon, instead verifying that they could all tread water and swim certain strokes for given distances. Everyone had passed, although Ben and Nicole were both pretty sketchy on the butterfly and Nicole had kept stopping to adjust her top every five seconds. Former water polo player Miguel had been their star, with strokes more expert than Ken's.

"Well, at least we got the swimming skills part over with. That's something," she said. "When we meet again this Saturday, we can get right down to business."

"I guess."

Finished with his hair, Jesse started drying his body. Melanie adjusted the striped towel she had wrapped around her own, trying to think of something clever to say but drawing a blank.

"You'll be here on Saturday, right?" she asked at last

He looked up again. "Of course."

"Okay. Well, I guess I'll see you Saturday, then. I mean, unless I run into you at school or something."

"All right."

She knew she should take advantage of the chance to make a graceful exit, but there was something about the way he was looking at her that froze her to the spot. Their gazes locked. She tried to push her feelings up into her eyes, to show him she was still crazy about him . . .

"Did you need a ride home or something?" he asked. "I'd take you, but I've got something else—"

"What? No!" she said, startled to be so misunderstood. "Leah's driving me. In fact, I'd better hurry and catch her."

She turned and started jogging toward the cabin before he could guess how foolish she felt. She had gone only a few feet, though, when he called out after her.

"See you Saturday!"

"Saturday!" she called back, not turning around in case he saw the grin all over her face.

Leah was standing in the cabin doorway, wearing shorts and a T-shirt soaked at the shoulders from contact with her wet hair. "There you are!" she exclaimed. "I thought you'd be right behind me."

"Sorry. I was just talking to Jesse."

"What about?" Leah asked, eyeing her a little suspiciously. "And why did it put you in such a good mood?"

"What? I'm not," Melanie said quickly. "I mean, Jesse's in a good mood. For once. I guess it just rubbed off."

Leah smiled knowingly, and for a moment Melanie thought she was busted. Then Leah said the last thing she expected.

"Don't tell anyone else, but I think Jesse has a girlfriend."

"Wh—what?" Melanie stammered. "Who?"

Leah glanced around to make sure no one was listening. Everyone else had already cleared out.

"Miguel says that all of a sudden Jesse is grocery shopping for Charlie Johnson nearly every day. It's like his new favorite activity or something."

"And?" Melanie prompted, not seeing the connection.

"And he always goes to the same convenience store, even though the grocery store is closer and cheaper. Jesse won't admit it, but from what he's let slip, Miguel thinks he has a crush on the checkout girl. Isn't that cute?"

"Cute," Melanie echoed weakly, breaking into goose bumps all over her body. The air temperature seemed to have suddenly plunged ten degrees, and she shivered inside her wet towel.

"You're freezing!" Leah exclaimed. "Why didn't you say so? Go get changed, and I'll wait for you by the trail."

Leah left, and Melanie slid the cabin door latch shut to make sure no one else came in. Instead of dressing, though, she leaned her wet head into the wood, letting a few hot tears mix with the cold lake water still trickling out of her hair.

It's only a rumor. A suspicion. You don't know anything for sure, she told herself over and over. Even so, she couldn't stop crying.

If Leah was right, she had waited too long.

She had just lost her chance.

Again.

Six

"You're working *again*? You worked last night." As hard as Leah had lobbied for Miguel to keep his part-time job at the hospital after Zach Dewey's death, she didn't dare complain, but she couldn't keep the wistfulness out of her voice either. "I wanted to do something tonight."

Miguel put down his sandwich and shrugged. "I thought you'd be studying for finals anyway."

"And you should be studying too. Why can't we study together?"

"You know that never works."

Something on the other side of the quad seemed to suddenly catch his attention. "What are all those people doing?"

From where they were sitting, on a concrete planter at the edge of CCHS's packed central quad, Leah could see people in every direction. She could only assume he was referring to the slightly thicker crowd around two tables outside the main building. "You mean the ones buying tickets for the senior picnic?"

"Is that all?" he said, returning to his sandwich.

Leah eyed the half-eaten slice of pizza in her lap, suddenly reminded of the dinner invitation Shane had made her two days before. She hadn't gone, of course, but now she half wondered why not. At least Shane seemed to enjoy her company. The way Miguel had been acting lately, it was hard to believe he'd have cared even if she'd told him all about it.

"What do you mean, is that all?" she asked. "We're going, aren't we?"

Miguel made a face. "How much does it cost?"

"Five dollars."

"Per person? That's too much."

That's nothing!" she said, astonished. "It costs almost that much to buy lunch here."

Miguel held up the crusts from his peanut butter and jelly. "That's why I don't buy lunch here."

"Miguel, it's the senior picnic," she said, hearing the whine in her voice. "I'll buy your ticket for you."

"Don't even think about it," he said. "I have the money, Leah. I'm just saving it for more important things."

"Like what? What's more important than graduation? These are our very last days of high school, Miguel. Don't you want to make them count?"

"I'm counting them, believe me."

"Miguel!"

"Fine. I'll buy a stupid ticket."

"Gee, don't do me any favors," she said sullenly.

"*Now* what's the problem? I thought you wanted me to go."

"*I* want you to *want* to go!" she corrected, exasperated.

"So then you *don't* want me to go? I'm confused."

"I can't even believe we're having this conversation!" Curious heads were beginning to turn, but Leah ignored the onlookers. "This is our *senior year*, Miguel, and we're barely doing *anything* together. Between your job, and Eight Prime, and now finals, it's like I hardly see you at—"

"All right, I get it. I'll go to the picnic. I *want* to go," he added before she could cut in. "I was just trying to save some money, that's all."

"Five dollars?" Leah said incredulously. "For something you'll remember all your life?"

"I just . . . If I'm going to buy Charlie's house, I need to get the down payment somewhere."

"Oh, now you're just kidding me! Five bucks is going to keep you from buying a house?"

"It has to come from somewhere," he repeated stubbornly.

"Does your mother even know about this yet?" Leah demanded. "What does she think of your plan?"

"I'll tell her when I feel like it. And why are you still arguing with me, anyway? I said I'd go."

A million retorts sprang to mind, but Leah bit her tongue. She didn't want to start a fight now, so close to graduation. There were only a day and a half left in the current week, then one more week, and that was it. After that she and Miguel would be out of high school forever. She didn't want to miss a minute of fun by fighting.

It's better just to drop it, she counseled herself, although taking her own advice was hard. Especially when she still had so much more she wanted to say.

That stupid house, she thought, suspecting it was the real reason he had so little time for her lately. The extra shifts at the hospital suddenly made perfect sense. *Why couldn't he have found out about it a month from now? Or, better still, after I leave for Stanford?*

He was never going to come up with that kind of money—what teenager could? But she knew him well enough to know that he'd drive himself crazy trying.

And me, she added, feeling half crazy already.

They would only be high school seniors once. This was their only chance to participate in commencement, the grad night trip to the amusement park, and all the senior activities. This was the culmination of their entire high school careers—of their entire childhoods, really.

Why can't he just enjoy it?

"Peter! Hey, Peter, wait up!" Melanie called, running to catch him after school on Thursday. His blue

Toyota was just a few spaces away in the student parking lot.

"Hi, Melanie. What's up? Need a ride?"

"No." A pained expression twisted her face. "Well, yeah. I *always* need a ride. But I can take the bus. I just wanted to ask you something."

Peter grinned. "I've got to get home fast, because we're all leaving in an hour for my brother's graduation. If you want, though, I can swing past your house on the way and you can ask me in the car."

"Okay. Thanks."

Peter opened the passenger door, letting out a blast of the superheated air inside. "The worst thing about hot weather is cars with dark interiors," he said, fanning the door back and forth.

"I'll bet Jesse's is even hotter," Melanie said, trying not to sound wistful. "He has that black leather."

"Miguel has vinyl. That's the worst, because once you start sweating you just slide around in the puddle."

"Peter!" she groaned. "Gross."

"You started it."

"I don't think so."

"Have a seat," he said with a smile, gesturing her into the car.

"I'm almost afraid to now."

"Oh, yeah. Because no one ever sits on the *bus* in shorts. Who even knows what's on *those* seats?"

Melanie laughed, mostly to avoid thinking about it. Until she turned sixteen and got her driver's license, she couldn't afford to develop an aversion to the bus. *More of an aversion, anyway.*

Peter climbed in too, and soon they were on the road. "So what's up?" he asked. "What did you want to ask me?"

"We, um, have water safety again on Saturday, right?" She knew they did, but Peter's directness had made her suddenly shy about asking her real question.

"Right."

"Do you think you can make Ben wear a belt this time?"

Peter laughed. "How about suspenders? That would be stylish."

"Make sure they're red and he'll probably jump on it," she said with a roll of her eyes.

"I don't think you need to worry about Ben. After yesterday's disaster, I'll bet he lies low for a while."

"You mean you hope he does."

He nodded. "It *would* be a relief to get those certifications behind us. It doesn't seem like people are taking this very seriously—especially with camp just a week away."

"It's not that people aren't serious. It's just that right now all anyone can think about is summer vacation."

"You're right. I probably should have left an empty week between the end of school and the start of camp. But those kids need a place to go, and I wanted to be there for them so—"

"It'll be fine," she said. "Don't worry."

Peter smiled. "That's what I keep telling Jenna."

An open field of grass appeared on Melanie's side of the car. They were almost to her house.

"You remember that time you said you'd lend me a study Bible?" she blurted out, afraid of losing her chance. "What exactly *is* that?"

If Peter was surprised, he didn't let it show.

"Well, there are all different kinds," he answered. "But basically it's a regular Bible with wide margins where they put the questions most people have, and they print the answers there too. Mine has maps, and tables, and time lines . . . things to help explain the difficult parts or highlight the key points. It's kind of like having a tutor there to help you understand what you're reading."

"That does sound helpful," Melanie said, nodding slowly. "I've been trying to read the New Testament, but I just don't get it at all. I honestly think there might be something wrong with my mom's old Bible—aside from the old-fashioned language, I mean. It's like they printed it wrong or something. I'm on the third guy now, and the thing just keeps repeating itself, practically word for word. It's worse than déjà vu."

Peter gave her a shocked look, then choked back a sudden laugh.

"What?"

"I'm sorry," he said, obviously struggling to wipe the smile off his face. "I've just never met anyone like you before, who was trying to read the Bible all on her own—"

"I'm about to quit," she said, stung by his laughter.

"No, don't quit!" he said, instantly serious. "We have study Bibles all over our house. I'll find a good one and bring it to you when I get back. You can keep it as long as you want."

Melanie's feelings were still hurt. "You don't have to."

"I want to. You'll be amazed how much clearer things are."

"Well . . . only if you want to," she said grudgingly.

"I do. And I can clear up that repetition thing for you right now. Remember how I said the Bible isn't one big book? That it's actually a bunch of ancient manuscripts, written by different people at different times? Those four books at the beginning of the New Testament—Matthew, Mark, Luke, and John—are called the Gospels. They do tell essentially the same story—the story of Jesus' life on Earth—but from four different viewpoints because they're written by four different people."

"But Peter, it's word for word," she protested.

Peter shook his head. "They're similar, but they

aren't identical. The study Bible will help you figure out what makes each one unique. It's kind of like when the police go somewhere and interview witnesses. Even if everyone saw the same thing, the story still differs slightly from person to person. People just remember different things, or think different things are important."

"So you're saying those four guys—Matthew, Luke, and the other two—actually saw all that stuff?"

"No. Matthew and John did. Luke and Mark heard the stories from other people."

"I am so confused," she said, feeling overwhelmed. If a person had to know all that just to make sense of the Bible, no wonder she was lost. "Maybe I should give up."

"No, try the study Bible. I promise it's going to make sense. And if it doesn't, ask me anything. If I don't know the answer, I'll find out."

"Yeah?"

He smiled, that reassuring Peter smile that had once made her fall half in love with him. "Of course. You bet."

"I've never eaten here before," Guy said, looking around the restaurant Nicole had brought him to for dinner. "What kind of food do they have?"

"Salads."

"And?"

"Well . . . soup, I think. Everyone comes for the salads."

Guy's eyes traveled the restaurant again, his skeptical expression calling attention to its emptiness.

"It's early," Nicole said defensively.

The only reason she had even invited him out that evening was because Jenna had made her feel guilty about drooling over Ken the afternoon before. Not that she wouldn't have gotten around to seeing Guy again eventually. Of course she would have. But she had kind of been waiting for him to call her. . . .

Until Jenna had made her think there was something wrong with that.

Jenna can be so old-fashioned sometimes. It's not as if Guy and I are engaged. Or going steady. Or even dating regularly.

She'd called him once since he had taken her to her prom, hoping to get together, but he'd been busy that whole weekend, camping with his family. He still didn't even know she was a cheerleader.

Unless Jeff told him. If Jeff knows.

Guy hadn't said anything about cheerleading when she called, though, so she didn't think that had happened. Still, the likelihood of his eventually getting the news secondhand was another reason she had asked Guy to dinner that Thursday. She wanted to tell him herself.

Not that I expect he'll be thrilled.

Guy had made his negative feelings about cheerleading clear. On the other hand, he had seemed genuinely sorry for her when she'd missed making the squad the first time, so maybe he would surprise her with a little enthusiasm.

"Don't they have any steaks or burgers or *anything*?" he asked.

"Some of the salads have meat in them. Wait for the menu," Nicole advised. "Oh, look, here comes the waitress now."

The woman put down glasses of water and handed them menus before walking off again. Nicole watched as Guy scanned his with a disappointed expression.

Other men like salad. Why can't he keep an open mind? she thought, annoyed.

But deep down she had known all along it was a mistake to bring him there. When he had taken her to dinner, they'd gone to meat-and-potatoes places, the type where food was served on platters instead of plates. She should have guessed that salad wouldn't be his idea of a satisfying meal.

"I had the chicken Caesar here once," Nicole ventured. "It's really big. You could order that with a side of garlic bread."

He looked skeptical.

"And soup."

Still unconvinced.

"And dessert," she added desperately. "That ought to fill you up."

He finally shrugged. "I'll give it a try. We can always go out for ice cream later."

When the waitress came back, Nicole ordered what seemed like half the menu for Guy and a small garden salad for herself. "With the low-cal Italian on the side. Make sure they put it on the *side*," she admonished. "And no croutons."

"Gee, that sounds thrilling," Guy said when the woman had left. "That's your whole dinner?"

"That's all I want," Nicole lied. "I need to stay in top condition now."

Interest sparked in his blue eyes. He leaned toward her across the table, his russet bangs falling into his face. "What for?"

"I'm on the cheerleading squad!" she announced triumphantly. "Somebody dropped out, and I moved into her place."

"Oh," he said, leaning back. "That's good. I guess. I mean, it's what you wanted. Right?"

"It's *all* I wanted."

"Well, then I'm happy for you. I guess."

If it wasn't a glowing endorsement, at least he hadn't said anything horrible. He was actually taking the news pretty well, considering how shallow he thought cheerleading was.

"Thank you," she said, pleased.

The food came then and they both dug in, so for a while Nicole didn't notice that the conversation had halted. But when her salad was long gone and Guy was starting on his pie, she could no longer ignore the silence. Maybe her announcement hadn't gone over quite as well as she'd thought.

"You know there's a creek out behind this place," she ventured, averting her eyes from his whipped cream. "It runs the whole length of the street before it veers back into the woods."

"Yeah," he said, interested. "Any fish?"

"I don't know. We could look."

Guy glanced toward the restaurant windows. "It's still plenty light. Let's do it."

Nicole paid the bill with the saved allowance she'd brought, trying not to notice how much more Guy's dinner had cost than her own or to think about the makeup and magazines she could have bought with the money instead. After all, she reminded herself, going out had been her idea, and he had always paid for them both in the past. They walked out through the back parking lot and over a stretch of weedy, unkempt ground. Nicole heard the creek before she saw it, the gurgling water blending with the traffic noise from the street until one sound gradually became the other.

"Hey, the stream's pretty wide right here," Guy announced, walking ahead and beating her to the bank. "And there's a good place to climb down."

He disappeared over the edge before the top of his head popped back up. "Come on. I'll give you a hand."

The path Guy had taken was narrow and steep. Nicole's new sandals were strappy and slick. She was glad of his steadying hand as she picked her way down to the water's edge. Trees closed over their heads, hiding them from the rest of the world, and clumps of wildflowers bloomed on the banks. The creek sang over the rocks at their feet. Nicole caught her breath at the unexpected romance of the place. For a second, it was almost as if they were back at the prom, back into the moment before Courtney had ruined their chance at a first kiss, back into each other. . . .

And then Guy dropped her hand.

"There could be some fish in these pools. Hard to say." Stepping out onto a rock, he peered into the water. "If we look hard enough, we might spot something."

"Do you think so?" Nicole asked, trying to sound interested. She wasn't. Not in the least.

Why is he talking about fish when he could finally be kissing me? Do we have to start back at square one every time we see each other?

Things had felt so different at the prom. For an hour or two they had seemed really close; now there was all sorts of distance between them again.

Nicole sighed. Maybe it was partly her fault. After all, Guy had definitely been about to kiss her before Courtney broke things up. As weird as his ideas about intimacy were, who knew how long it would take him to work back up to that moment? Not to mention that finding out he was now dating a cheerleader had probably thrown him for a loop. Her position in the world had changed a lot, and even someone as unworldly as Guy had to recognize that.

As she watched him hop from rock to rock, his attention on the water, an odd set of emotions flowed through her. Part of her thought he had never looked cuter, part of her was truly sad that they'd lost ground, and part of her wanted to scream with impatience.

Does he want to be my boyfriend or not? Because it's not like I need him anymore.

She was glad of the good times they'd had, but if their relationship wasn't going anywhere . . .

Now that I'm a cheerleader, I can replace him in ten seconds.

Seven

"No shoving! Get back in your chairs right now!" Mrs. Wilson barked. "If I don't get some co-operation, you can forget about seeing these today."

The crowd in Jenna's homeroom dispersed instantly, people practically running to their seats in their desire not to irk the teacher into withholding their yearbooks.

"She has to pass them out today. Right?" Cyn Girard whispered nervously to Jenna. "I mean, she can't really keep them until Monday. I'll die!"

"Me too," Jenna admitted.

It wasn't waiting three more days so much as the fact that the whole rest of the school would have theirs. People would be studying them in every class, passing them around and getting signatures. At lunch, yearbooks were all anyone would talk about. If Jenna's homeroom didn't get theirs, they'd look like a bunch of rejects.

"All right, we'll try this one more time. And since you can't take turns walking up here like adults, we'll do it alphabetically." Mrs. Wilson consulted a list that had come with the books. "Carver . . . Conrad . . . Evans . . ."

Jenna hurried forward to take a yearbook from the box, so intent on getting back to her seat that she didn't hear the names Mrs. Wilson continued to call. The yearbook's cover was green embossed with gold, and Jenna could barely wait to see what its pages held. A big chunk was always taken up with the official portrait of every student in school, but there would also be pages and pages devoted to clubs and sports and events throughout the year. Best of all were the candids, the photographs taken of unknowing victims during the course of a normal day. Those were always funny: a jock putting on Chap Stick like lipstick, a popular beauty yawning without covering her mouth, someone adjusting their underwear . . . A person couldn't laugh too hard, though, until she made sure none of the shots were of her.

Jenna dropped into her chair and was about to open her yearbook when she noticed Miguel in the row to her right. There was nothing at all on his desk, and his eyes were fixed straight ahead.

"Miller . . . ," the teacher read. "O'Brien . . ."

"Hey, Miguel!" Jenna whispered to him across the aisle. "Where's your yearbook? Did Mrs. Wilson forget to call you?"

He shrugged. "I didn't order one this year. The price was a total rip-off."

"But it's your senior year!" Jenna knew money was tight for Miguel, but she was unable to believe he would pass on something so important. "They always order a few extra. If you hurry, you can probably buy one at the office today. I have ten dollars, and Jesse always has money. I'm sure Leah—"

"You don't get it, Jenna. I have the money. I'm just saving it for more important things."

"Like—like what?"

"Like lots of stuff," he said, a little impatiently. "A new place to live, for one. We'll be moving pretty soon."

Turning his eyes forward, he settled lower in his chair, his large hands gripping the edges of his desktop. "The sooner the better," he muttered.

She felt like arguing with him—if he'd been Peter, she'd have argued all day. But Miguel kept his life so private that Jenna was afraid she had already intruded too much. Reluctantly she let the subject drop, tearing her eyes away from the back of his head to focus on her own desk again. Her brand-new yearbook lay in front of her, still unopened, but for the moment it had lost its fascination.

I am so lucky that all I have to worry about is being a teenager, she thought, trying to imagine Miguel's life. Most days just growing up seemed hard enough for her. Working to help support a family was so far outside her experience that she could barely guess what it would be like. Anytime Jenna picked up a baby-sitting job or found another way to make money, she always kept it all for herself, pooling it with her allowance to spend on books and CDs and movies and whatever else she wanted.

Miguel probably doesn't even get an allowance, she realized for the first time, *and the money he earns he's saving for rent*. The knowledge made her feel suddenly childish, and selfish, and sheltered.

And grateful.

Somebody ought to buy him a yearbook. Except that Miguel was so proud sometimes, it was hard to know if he'd take it. *Maybe I'll talk to Leah about it at lunchtime. If I can catch her alone*.

Peter wasn't at school that day, having left with his parents the evening before to attend David's graduation, so Jenna was going to need someone else to eat with anyway.

I wish he were here, she thought with a pang, missing him already. Peter would know what to do about Miguel. Not to mention how much more fun it would be to go through the yearbook with him than alone. *Maybe I'll save it until he gets back*, she thought, slipping the unopened book into her pack. *He'll be back tomorrow for water safety, and that's not that far away. We can look at it after class*.

"Jenna, you have to sign my yearbook!" Cyn said, shoving the open volume at her from across the aisle. "You can be first. Sign anywhere you want."

"Oh, um, okay." Jenna pulled her own book out of her backpack again. "Do you want to sign mine?"

Cyn took Jenna's book, flipped it open, and began scribbling, while Jenna looked down at Cyn's. JUNIORS, the open page proclaimed over a collage of candid shots. Jenna smiled, both with relief at not finding any embarrassing photographs of herself and at the realization that she wouldn't be a junior much longer.

Next year, seniors! she thought dreamily, beginning to turn pages in search of the perfect place to sign. She tried not to see what was on them, still wanting to wait for Peter . . . but how could she choose a place without looking?

Peter will understand, she thought, flipping more slowly. *Besides, what else am I going to do at lunch?*

Okay, there they are. Nicole had spotted the other new cheerleaders in the cafeteria. *Stay calm and act like it's no big deal.*

She gripped her yearbook with both hands, working up her nerve.

The old cheerleading squad, including Melanie, Tanya, Lou Anne, and Angela, still ate lunch together. The other members of the new squad had started hanging out in their own group, though, and they were Nicole's target that Friday. The six had a table near the center of the cafeteria, and more yearbooks than lunches were spread across its surface as they chatted about various pages and took turns signing for each other. Nicole slowly began walking toward them, planning to ask them to sign hers, too.

This will break the ice, she reassured herself as she threaded through the tables. *Besides, I have every right to sit with them. They might like me if they gave me a chance.*

"Candi Adams ought to be dying right now," Nicole heard Debbie say as she closed the last few feet. "That outfit is *so* last year."

"Not to mention the color," Sidney Wallace added. "What could she have been thinking?"

Jamila Kane glanced at the photo they were studying and rolled her eyes. "Wannabes!" she exhaled.

Nicole's steps faltered a second as she imagined what they said about *her*. Then she forced herself to take the plunge and break in on the conversation.

"Hi!" she said brightly. "What are you all doing?"

She knew she should have thought of a better question the moment they looked at her. "I mean, signing yearbooks, huh?" she said, trying to cover her own stupidity. "I just got mine, too."

"I'm pretty sure the whole school did," Debbie said sarcastically.

Sidney snorted. Maria Martinez rolled her eyes, then looked away. The other girls followed suit, returning their attention to the yearbooks on the table. Nicole's heart sank. How was she going to ask to join them if they wouldn't even look at her?

I should leave, she thought, her palms growing slick against the cover of her yearbook. *And I should do it now, before this gets any more embarrassing. I'll just take my book and go find—*

"Do you want to sit with us?" Kara Tibbs offered unexpectedly. She slid over on the bench, opening up a space between her and Becca Harvey, the girl who had squeaked onto the squad in the number ten spot—right before Nicole.

"I, um, yeah," Nicole said, climbing into the gap. Her stomach was full of butterflies as she settled onto the bench, but she tried to calm them by telling herself she had cleared the first big hurdle. At least she was part of the group now.

Sort of.

"So. You guys are signing yearbooks." She opened her own to one of several blank pages in front. "That's perfect, because I want you all to sign mine. See? I saved a blank page just for the squad."

"It looks like you saved a lot of blank pages," Jamila observed.

Debbie snickered. "You want us *all* to sign? I mean . . . we barely know you, Nicole."

"Well, but . . . you're *going* to know me. Really well," Nicole countered, feeling desperate again.

"I'll sign it," Kara said, grabbing for the book. Her pen had one of those childish cartoon erasers on the end, but by then Nicole was prepared to cut her all kinds of slack. Kara was the only girl on the squad who had been nice to her at all.

"Here you go," she said, pushing the book back to Nicole.

Nicole tried to pretend she wasn't reading, but she couldn't resist skimming the short lines of pink ink.

To Nicole:
Next year will be fun. Have a good summer. See you at camp!
Kara Tibbs

It wasn't Shakespeare, but those few words made Nicole feel so much better.

"Here, give it to me," Debbie said unexpectedly, reaching for Nicole's yearbook.

Nicole froze, shocked, then pushed it toward her eagerly. She wasn't sure exactly how Debbie had become the ringleader of the new girls, but it seemed pretty clear that she had. Maybe it was because Debbie had placed right behind Tanya and Melanie in the tryouts—or maybe there was something about her attitude that made the others afraid to cross her. Whatever the reason, if Debbie signed Nicole's yearbook, everyone else was sure to follow.

"Do you want to use my pen?" Nicole offered.

"I think I've got it covered," Debbie said, raising the pen already in her hand. Her eyebrows were raised as well, warning Nicole that she was acting too eager again.

"It's just that I have this new one . . . one that writes really smooth . . . I just thought . . ."

Debbie scrawled something quickly and pushed the open book back to Nicole.

Nicole—
Good luck!
Debbie Morris

*　*　*

To a pretty girl and a rad cheerleader—
Melanie, it was fun having you in English this year. I only wish our chairs had been closer. (ha ha) See you next year. Stay cool!
Paul Eckert

Dear Melanie,
What will you do without me next year? I know what I'll be doing—college! I still can't believe you dropped out of the cheerleading squad. I bet you'll be sorry. Can you believe you still have two whole years of school left to go? I'm so glad I'm a senior!
See you around,
Tiffany Barrett

Hey, Melanie, you traitor!
I have plenty of things I want to say to you, but most

of them probably shouldn't be in writing. (Just kidding ☺)
I still just can't accept that you're not going to be on the
squad next year. It won't be the same without you! Let's
get together this summer. Call me.

Love, Tanya

Hey, Melanie,
I saw you at all the games this year. You were awe-
some. Maybe we'll have some classes together next year.
Jeff Horner

"Hasn't *anyone* noticed that I'm a person and not
just a cheerleader?" Melanie asked her empty bedroom, throwing her yearbook aside in disgust. "I'm
glad I quit the squad, if that's the only way people
think of me."

She had been leafing through the new yearbook for
the past hour that Friday night, memorizing its pages.
She appeared on a surprising number, actually, and
not exclusively in her cheerleader's uniform. She was
all over the candid pages: smiling, smiling, smiling.

*Anyone who didn't know better would think I was
having fun.*

Which had been exactly her intention when
she'd faked all those smiles. Still . . .

*I didn't know I was such a good faker. I mean, I knew
I was fake, but not that fake.*

Was it possible she'd been having more fun than
she remembered?

I guess cheerleading was all right. Sometimes. At least it got me out of the house.

She glanced over the edge of her bed and down at her floor, as if she could see through to her father downstairs, sleeping off another beer-induced coma. Then, rolling over on the blankets, she picked up her yearbook again and flipped to a page that was already becoming familiar.

The photograph captured the first frantic moments after the football team's season-opening win against Springville, the one where Jesse had caught that wild final pass. He had pulled off his helmet to gloat; his brown hair framed his face in sweaty spikes. But it was his eyes that held her attention. There was something so triumphant in his expression, so full of life, so . . . Jesse.

God, I miss him.

Was he really seeing someone new? Aside from Leah's saying so, Melanie hadn't seen any evidence. Which didn't mean it wasn't true . . .

She slammed the yearbook shut. Considering how much she had looked forward to getting it, she was finding it surprisingly depressing. She decided to try her mother's Bible again instead.

Now that Peter explained that Gospels thing to me, maybe it will make more sense, she thought hopefully, removing a bookmark from between delicate pages. She made herself comfortable on the bed and resumed reading from the Gospel of Luke:

And he spake also a parable unto them; No man putteth a piece of a new garment upon an old; if otherwise, then both the new maketh a rent, and the piece that was taken out of the new agreeth not with the old. And no man putteth new wine into old bottles; else the new wine will burst the bottles, and be spilled, and the bottles shall perish. But new wine must be put into new bottles; and both are preserved. No man also having drunk old wine straightway desireth new: for he saith, the old is better.

Melanie groaned and let her head loll back in her pillows. *Is that even English? If God wants people to believe in him, then why is he so hard to understand?*

Peter had promised to bring her that study Bible, but he wouldn't be back from David's graduation until tomorrow. In the meantime . . .

She read the passage again, then slammed the Bible shut as well.

Maybe there's something on TV.

Eight

"I hope people are going to pay attention this time," Jenna told Peter as they hurried across the clearing. He had only just arrived at the campground, back from David's graduation, but it was already time to join the rest of Eight Prime and Ken over on the benches.

"I'm sure they will," Peter said. "Everyone must realize this is getting down to the wire now."

Jenna grabbed one of his arms, stopping him under the big central oak. "Just in case, I think we ought to have a plan."

Peter grinned. "What kind of plan?"

"An anti-messing-around plan."

"Sounds official."

"Peter! I'm serious."

"Why don't we play it by ear?" he said, glancing toward the waiting group. "If people don't pay attention, then we'll come up with something."

"Okay. They'd better."

The two of them started walking again.

"David's supposed to stop by later," Peter said. "I hope he gets here in time to meet everyone."

"But he already met them, at the work party we had to clean this place up."

"That was a long time ago. He's afraid he won't recognize everyone or remember people's names."

"I bet he remembers Ben," Jenna said darkly. "If he doesn't, he will after today."

Peter chuckled. "No doubt. Come on, let's hurry."

Over at the benches, Jenna was surprised to see that nearly everyone had brought a yearbook. Even Ken was poring over the pages, laughing at candids of total strangers.

"Hi, Peter," said Melanie. "How was your trip?"

"Good. They passed out the yearbooks, huh?"

"I wanted to pick yours up for you," Jenna told him. "But they wouldn't let me."

"I'll get it on Monday," Peter said, unconcerned.

"You can look at mine if you want," Melanie offered. "I want you to sign it anyway." She began to hand it over, but Jenna intervened.

"We can all do yearbooks later," she said, loudly enough for everyone to hear. "We don't want to waste Ken's time."

"We're not wasting your time," said Nicole, inching closer to Ken on the bench. Apparently the yearbook in his lap was hers. "Are we?" she added, leaning boldly against his bare shoulder.

"No. It's cool," he said, turning another page.

"Well, but we have a lot to do. We ought to get started," Jenna insisted uneasily, wanting to get off to a good start for once.

"Yeah, I need to get out of here," said Miguel. "I'm working at the hospital this afternoon, so the sooner we finish, the better."

"Oh, definitely. You wouldn't want to be late for the hospital," said Leah.

Jenna thought she sounded kind of cranky.

"You know what we should do?" Ben proposed, sitting up straighter on the bench. "Let's have a swimming race to see who's fastest."

"It's Miguel," said Jesse. "Why even race?"

"Okay, then," Ben said. "Who's *second* fastest?"

"Why do you care?" asked Nicole. "It's not you."

"Probably Jesse," said Ken.

Jesse shrugged. "I'll bet I couldn't beat you."

Ken smiled and turned a page. "I'll bet you couldn't either."

"I'd like to try, though," Jesse said, a competitive spark in his eyes. "Why don't we make it best two out of three?"

"Why don't we get our certifications first?" Jenna said, trying unsuccessfully to keep the testiness out of her voice. "Then you can all race as much as you want to."

"Oh, look! That's my back!" Nicole squealed proudly, pointing to a picture for Ken. "The redhead is my best friend, Courtney."

"Are you sure?" Leah asked, leaning over to see.

"Of course I'm sure! No one else at school has hair like that."

"No, that's obviously Courtney. Are you sure that's *you*?" Leah shook her head. "I don't think so."

Melanie stood up and walked over. "Let me see it."

Nicole handed her the open book.

Ken turned to face Jesse. "You really think you can beat me?"

"Are you so sure I can't?"

"Can we just do this?" Jenna shouted. "Can we *please* do water safety?"

Everyone turned to stare—even Peter. Their shocked expressions made her realize how shrewish she had sounded.

"Well, I'm sorry, but we're wasting time," she said defensively. "And I thought Miguel was in a hurry to leave."

She turned to him, hoping for backup, but Miguel just shrugged.

"I probably don't need to be here for the whole thing anyway," he said. "You all know I can swim. And if I ever have to rescue anyone, I'll just grab them and pull them out. No big deal."

No big deal? Jenna imagined steam coming out her ears, like one of those silly cartoon characters.

"If we don't have our certifications, the park won't let us have the camp," she said tightly. "So how about putting the yearbooks away and getting serious? For once."

"Geez. Who put the bug up your butt?" Jesse muttered as he rose to his feet and shed the towel around his shoulders. "Last I knew, we were waiting for you and Peter."

Jenna flinched a bit as she realized the truth of his statement.

Ken stood up as well, looking embarrassed. "I was just . . . I certainly didn't mean to waste anyone's time."

"No, it's *your* time we're wasting," Jenna tried to explain.

"Let's just get started," said Peter. "Is everybody ready?"

"Yes," the group said in unison, giving Jenna offended looks.

She closed her eyes and took a deep breath. *Okay, so maybe I was a little out of control. But somebody has to take charge.*

"Let's go down to the dock," Ken said. "We'll start with rescue entries, then move on to surface dives." He picked up a long red rectangle of foam, slinging its strap over his shoulder. "Did you get the rescue tubes yet, Peter?"

Peter shook his head. "Sorry. I've been out of town. But I'll have them next class, I promise."

"We're going to need those to practice rescues."

"I know," Peter said sheepishly. "Can we use yours for today?"

Jenna started walking toward the dock without waiting to hear Ken's answer. Now even Peter was messing up. *And he's the one who ought to care the most!*

She couldn't have said exactly why she was so upset. She still expected Eight Prime to get its certificates somehow. She just hated looking so unmotivated and disorganized in front of an outsider. *Even if Ken isn't exactly Mr. Efficiency himself.*

Still, that's not the point, she argued. *If we're supposed to be in charge of kids all summer, we shouldn't be acting like we need baby-sitters ourselves!*

"Are you going to Leah's birthday party tomorrow night?" Melanie asked Jesse.

He stopped toweling his hair, leaving it sticking out all over like the picture in her yearbook. "I guess so. Aren't you?"

"I think everyone is. It ought to be fun."

Jesse glanced down toward the water. He and Melanie were at the benches, but the others were still fooling around on the shore.

"Are you sure?" he asked in a lowered voice. "Leah wasn't in a very good mood today, and Miguel said she hardly invited anyone to this thing besides Eight Prime."

Melanie saw an opportunity that had nothing to do with Leah's birthday. "That's right. Leah told me you and Miguel were hanging out a lot lately."

"Not really." He seemed confused. "I mean, we painted Charlie's house, but that was a while ago. We went by there later for a hammer. . . ." He shrugged, his eyes searching hers. "Is that what you meant?"

"I guess. I thought Leah said something about you grocery shopping for Charlie."

"Yeah, but not with Miguel. I don't know what she's talking about."

Nothing about his behavior hinted that he was nervous or embarrassed or trying to hide anything. He returned to toweling himself, focusing on the muscles of his chest and the long washboard expanse of his stomach. Melanie felt the water still running down her own skin, but the sensation barely registered compared to the rush of hope that the checkout-girl rumor was exactly that—a rumor.

"Did you forget your towel?" Jesse asked, giving her a questioning look.

"What? Oh." What else was he supposed to think, with her rooted to the spot, staring at his towel like a total idiot? At least she *hoped* he thought she was staring at his towel. "No. It's just up . . . over . . ." She pointed vaguely. "Did you buy Leah a present?"

"Were we supposed to?"

She shrugged. "It is a birthday party."

"Great. I don't know what girls like," he complained, draping his wet towel over the back of his neck. "I mean, I *know* what they . . . oh, forget it."

Melanie fought a smile. For Jesse to admit there was *anything* he didn't know about girls was a pretty big step.

"What did you get her?" he asked.

"Nothing yet. I'm shopping tomorrow."

"Really?" He lifted one eyebrow. "Want to go in on something with me? I'll pay for it if you go get it."

"You're that desperate to get out of shopping for a girl?"

He nodded. "Absolutely."

"Fine," she said with a smile. "But you just pay for your half."

"I don't mind—" he began.

"Jesse, I don't need your money."

An ironic expression crept into his eyes. "I guess we have at least *that* in common."

For a second she felt that old connection between them again—the one she dreamed of, the one she ached for . . .

Then he grabbed his towel with both hands, flipped it over his head, and snapped the end of it at her bare legs.

"Jesse!" she squealed. "Ow!"

"That didn't hurt. If you want it to hurt, you have to do it like this." He cocked the towel back to try again.

"Stop it!" she giggled, running away.

He chased her, but not fast, letting her keep an easy lead.

"Towel fight!" Ben shouted, spotting the action. He began running up from the shore while trying to twist his towel into a weapon, nearly tripping over his shoelaces in the process.

Melanie ran past a bench and managed to grab her own towel. Making it into a rope, she turned and fired back at Jesse.

Soon everyone was in on the fun, damp towels flicking everywhere. Melanie knew that an aggressively wielded wet towel could do damage, but no one was trying to snap off flesh. The whole encounter was more like a wet pillow fight.

"I'll get you, Jesse!" Melanie cried, slapping at him with her towel.

"Is that a threat or a promise?" he asked, taking aim.

She laughed as she ran off again. Was it her imagination, or were they flirting?

I should just ask him about that checkout girl, she thought as her bare feet flew over the dirt. *Why not just ask him and get it behind us?*

But she was having fun—everyone was—and she didn't want to ruin the moment with an answer she might not want to hear.

There's no way he can keep something that big a secret anyway. If it's true, I'll find out sooner or later. And if it's not . . . then I'll definitely find some courage and tell him how I feel.

"I'm coming to get you, Andrews!" Jesse shouted.

I hope so, she thought with a smile.

"Happy birthday to you!" all of Leah's party guests finished singing together.

Leah tried to smile, but she was so embarrassed she could barely keep from running out of the room.

"I told you, no singing!" she hissed to her mom as Mrs. Rosenthal set a chocolate cake with eighteen glowing candles down in front of her at the head of the table.

"Jenna started it," Mrs. Rosenthal returned calmly. "Besides, it's over now. And hey, you survived!"

"Blow out the candles," Ben called from the other end of the long table.

The party was being held in the condominium building's recreation room, the Rosenthals having decided there was no comfortable way to entertain so many people in their small condo. All of Eight Prime was there, and so were Courtney Bell and Miguel's sister, Rosa. Leah had considered inviting a few more people from school, but in the end she had decided it would be more fun to keep to her closest friends.

"You have to make a wish," Jenna instructed.

Leah sucked in a deep breath, trying to come up with something fast. Once the candles were out, the cake could be cut and people would have something to do again besides look at her. She was on the verge of blowing out the candles and only pretending she'd wished when her eye caught Miguel's.

I wish he'd get more into school next week, she thought, beginning a long exhalation. *Not to mention more into me. I wish he would realize how little time we have left and start making the most of it.*

The candles were out. People clapped around the table.

Nicole picked up her blue plastic cup and held it aloft. "Cheers!" she said, swigging her iced tea.

The meal had been pizza and salad, and remnants of crusts on balloon-printed plates still littered the red tablecloth. Mr. Rosenthal started moving along behind the chairs, refilling people's drinks from pitchers of tea and punch.

"Do you want to cut the cake, or should I?" Leah's mother asked.

They decided to serve it up together so they could get the plates passed around faster. Everyone took big pieces except Nicole, who refused even one bite. Now that she was on the cheerleading squad, whatever obsessions she'd relaxed about her weight were apparently back in full force.

"Open your presents," Miguel urged.

Mr. Rosenthal put down the pitchers and checked his watch. "It is getting kind of late," he told Leah. "You can finish your cake afterwards."

Leah nodded, still stuffed anyway. She put her cake to one side and turned to the presents piled in a chair behind her. Since she had elected to have her party on her actual birthday instead of Friday or Saturday, she had known that people would need to leave early. Finals started tomorrow.

"Open the big bag first," Melanie directed, standing up to see better. "That one's from me and Jesse."

Leah lifted a printed gift bag by its purple string handles, removing the nest of shredded tissue that covered the contents. Inside was a collection of fancy bath salts and lotions, complete with a long back brush.

"I'll bet *you* picked this stuff out, right, Jesse?" Leah teased, lifting an exotic-looking soap to her nose. "Ooh, that smells *good*! Thanks, you two."

There was a book of jokes from Ben, and Nicole and Courtney had chipped in on a sleek black book bag.

"For next year," Nicole explained. "All the magazines are showing them."

Jenna's gift was handmade: a picture frame painted sky blue and decorated with seashells. "If we can get a good photo of Eight Prime all together, you can put us in there," she suggested.

"Open mine," Peter said. His gift was a disposable camera and a gift certificate for developing the pictures at a local camera store.

The final present was from Miguel. Leah smiled at

him as she untied the velveteen ribbon, wondering what could be inside. It was no accident she had saved his, the most special gift, for last. The box was only a little larger than a college dictionary, but surprisingly heavy for its size.

"What's in here? Rocks?" she joked, stripping off the paper.

It almost sounded as if Rosa muttered, "Rocks would be an improvement," but there was a lot of noise at the table.

Opening the box eagerly, Leah paused, confused, at the sight of what looked like a small plastic briefcase.

"Oh, it's a . . . a . . ."

"Open it," Miguel urged.

Leah fumbled with the stiff plastic clasps, finally managing to unsnap the lid. She opened the case with growing anticipation, only to sit staring dumbfounded at its contents.

"It's a tool kit!" said her boyfriend. "Everyone should have their own basic set of tools. Hanging up framed posters in your dorm room, fixing a leaky faucet . . . "

He half stood to lean across the table, pointing out the obvious. "See? You've got a hammer and both types of screwdrivers. There's your tape measure and a pair of pliers. You'll be surprised how much stuff you can fix with just those few things."

Surprised? Surprised didn't begin to cover it.

"Thanks, Miguel. How . . . um . . . handy," she heard herself saying into the silence that had descended over the table.

Leah's mother put a comforting hand on her shoulder. "You'll be surprised," she said.

There was that word again. Melanie and Nicole both shot her sympathetic looks.

"Now you have to open your present from your mother and me," Mr. Rosenthal said. "It was a little too hard to get through the door, so we left it just outside."

"Huh?" said Leah, still recovering from the romantic gift of tools. "I didn't see anything outside."

"You didn't?" Her father looked puzzled. "You didn't see that big package?"

"No."

"Oh, Joe. I hope nobody *took* it," Mrs. Rosenthal said worriedly.

Leah looked back and forth between her parents, not sure if they were kidding or not. Ben got up and sprinted to the open door.

"There's nothing out here," he reported, peering into the darkness. "I don't see a thing."

"That can't be," Mr. Rosenthal insisted, walking over to look himself.

Leah rose from her chair and followed. Everyone else crowded into the doorway behind her, trying to see over each other's heads into the night outside the rec room. The door opened onto a sidewalk bordered by a strip of barely lit landscaping. The only thing beyond the shrubs was the visitors' parking lot. Leah looked up and down the walkway, still not seeing anything that looked like a present.

"That's so weird," Mr. Rosenthal said. "I could have sworn I parked it . . ."

Leah felt her heart miss a beat.

"Yes! There it is," he said, pointing into the visitors' lot. "The one with the big bow on top."

"Daddy!" she squealed, spotting the outline of a car with a giant bow beneath a dim pole lamp. Not stopping for anyone else, she hurdled the bushes and tore across the asphalt. Halfway there she got her first good look and almost fell to her knees with the shock. The car was a brand-new Volkswagen Cabrio convertible, a dealer's sticker still inside the windshield.

"Oh!" she gasped, surprised by a rush of happy tears that squeezed her vocal cords shut. She could hear the others running up behind her as she stroked a gentle hand over the dark blue paint on the hood. "Oh!"

"Leah! Cool car! I can't wait until I learn to drive," Melanie added plaintively.

"Lucky!" Nicole accused enviously. "You are always so *lucky*, I swear!"

Everyone started talking at once, crowding

around to inspect the details and cupping their hands to peer into the windows. Leah looked to Miguel for a comment, but he just shook his head, speechless.

"Do you like it?" Mrs. Rosenthal asked, walking up last with Leah's father.

"Are you kidding? I love it!" Leah hugged both her parents fiercely, not caring that she was crying in front of her friends. "I wasn't expecting this at all. Not at *all*."

Mr. Rosenthal grinned. "I guess you'll want to keep it, then," he said, holding up a key on a long red ribbon.

"You'll need a car when you go off to school," her mother explained, "and so we thought, Why not get it now? This way you can enjoy it all summer."

"I just . . . I'm so . . . *thank* you," Leah stammered, overcome. "It must have been so expensive . . . and with tuition . . ."

Her father held up a hand. "We started saving for this the day we found out your mother was pregnant."

"Literally," Mrs. Rosenthal added playfully, poking her husband in the ribs. "I think we went straight from the doctor to the bank."

"Hey, Leah, take us for a ride!" Ben said.

"I can't take everyone," she replied hesitantly. "You won't all fit."

"Not to be a wet blanket," her father said, "but I'd rather you don't drive the car for the first time in the dark anyway. You need to get used to how it feels and where the controls are. You and I can get up early tomorrow and take it for a spin before school."

Leah nodded, relieved to have an excuse. The last thing she wanted was to put a ding in that perfect paint job.

"That doesn't mean you kids can't sit out here and listen to the stereo," Mrs. Rosenthal said. "I think you'll find some new CDs in the glove compartment."

Leah hugged both of her parents again before they returned to the rec room to start cleaning up. Then she unlocked the doors of her new car, and her friends took turns piling in, checking the upholstery and pressing random buttons.

"Put this CD in," Jesse said, handing her one from the glove compartment.

"Put the top down," Miguel suggested, finding his voice at last. "Then everyone can see."

They finally figured out how to retract the top, leaving the seats open to the stars. People took turns sitting behind the steering wheel, some clearly fantasizing about being the car's owner.

"This is so sweet," Peter said, turning the headlights off and on.

"Try the windshield wipers," Ben said, reaching for the controls.

"No!" Nicole and Courtney shouted from the back. "Do you want to get us all wet?"

Leah pulled Miguel over to the edge of the group. "So what do you think?" she asked.

"It's nice," he said, a little stiffly. "If I'd known you were getting a car, I could have got you the auto tool kit."

She wrapped her arms around him and brought her lips to his ear. "After everyone else goes home, maybe you and I can try out the backseat."

"I have to get home too," he said. "In fact, I ought to leave right now. I promised my mom not to keep Rosa late, plus there's that geometry final in the morning. I wouldn't mind getting in a couple more hours of cramming."

"*Everyone* has finals tomorrow. Stay just a little longer."

He kissed the top of her head. "I can't. But tomorrow, if you bring the car to school, I'll buy you lunch at Burger City. We can check it all out then."

Leah watched with a lump in her throat as Miguel rounded up his sister and said good-bye to their friends.

"I'll see you tomorrow," he promised, waving, as he and Rosa walked off.

"I should be going too," Jenna said. "I have a geometry final tomorrow."

"I know," Leah said dully.

The next minute everyone was remembering the finals they'd have to take the next day and saying their good-byes. Ben was the last to go, his hand lingering longingly on the Volkswagen's fender. "You'll definitely take me for a ride sometime, though. Right?" he asked.

"You've got it," she told him. "I promise."

Ben left, reassured, and Leah was still fooling around trying to get the top locked back into place when an unexpected voice outside the car's window almost gave her a heart attack.

"So this is what a Rosenthal gets for turning eighteen. Watch out for twenty-one!"

A mischievous grin in the darkness gave her mystery man away.

"Shane! What are you doing here?" she demanded, her heart up in her throat. "You scared me to death!"

"Sorry. I just saw your folks in the rec room and they said you were out here. I thought I'd come check out the new wheels."

His explanation made no sense at all. "But what are you doing *here?*" she repeated, climbing out of the car.

"Your dad mentioned that it was your birthday today, so I thought I'd crash your party." He looked around at the emptiness outside their little pool of light. "High school kids sure go to bed early these days! I could have shown you all a few things about how to party."

"It's finals week," Leah said irritably. She couldn't believe he'd had the nerve to come uninvited, let alone that her father had apparently helped him. "I was just getting ready to go in myself."

"All right. Peace," he said, holding up one palm. "Don't you want to open your birthday present?"

Producing a tiny box from inside his jacket, he held it out to her.

"For me?" She hadn't intended to sound suspicious, but she did. It was just that boxes that size tended to hold jewelry, as opposed to, say, screwdrivers and hammers.

"What is it? The world's smallest electric drill?" she joked uncomfortably.

Shane laughed. "Tools! Now, *that* would be a romantic gift! No. Go ahead, open it."

Leah opened the box with a sinking feeling, not wanting romance from Shane. Why couldn't *Miguel* have been thinking in terms of small boxes? Inside, curled on a white cotton pad, was a silver neck chain with a round, black-and-white enameled charm depicting the Chinese symbols for yin and yang.

"I thought you'd be into that cosmic balance stuff—philosophy major and all," Shane explained, moving closer. "Put it on."

Leah hesitated. "I . . . don't know if I should."

"What's the matter?" he asked. "Don't you like it?"

"I do." She liked it a lot, in fact. "It's just that . . . well . . . you don't know me well enough to give me jewelry."

She tried to hand the box back to Shane, but he only smiled—a lazy, amused kind of smile.

"That's kind of a judgment call, isn't it?"

Plucking the chain from the box, he opened the clasp and pulled its ends around her neck. His fingers were warm on her bare skin as he fastened the necklace beneath her hair. He had moved so close behind her that his body brushed against hers; she could feel his breath in her hair. She stiffened. Then relaxed. Then slowly leaned back against him.

"There," he said huskily, dropping the chain into place. "Maybe I know you better than you think."

Nine

"How about this test?" Jenna asked Miguel nervously. Geometry class was due to start any minute, and so was their first final. "Are you ready for it?"

Miguel shrugged. "As ready as I'll ever be. You?"

"I guess."

Jenna leaned back in her chair and chewed the end of her pencil nervously. She could feel her pulse twitching in her neck, and her feet had found a life of their own, tapping strange rhythms on the floor. All around her people had their faces buried in textbooks, desperately trying to soak up some last bit of knowledge that might improve their score. Notes were passed, example problems were argued, and the tapping of pencils built and built until it was almost the only sound in the room.

I don't have to be this scared, she thought, glancing at the clock and wondering why their teacher wasn't there yet. *I know I'm going to pass.*

She didn't want just to pass, though. She wanted to get an A.

"Jenna!" Miguel said, snapping her back to attention.

"Yeah?"

He smiled. "Good luck, okay?"

"Yeah. You too."

"I can barely believe we're already taking finals. The whole year went so fast."

"It did."

She might have said more, but Mrs. Wilson picked that moment to bustle through the doorway, a load of stapled test papers in one arm.

"Here we go," Jenna whispered, feeling her stomach lurch.

Miguel smiled again, flashing her two thumbs up before facing forward in his chair.

"I will take the roll," Mrs. Wilson said ceremoniously, as if she hadn't taken roll every morning all year.

"What for?" Doug Howell asked. "Anyone who isn't here is totally screwed anyway."

The nervous laughter dried up at the sight of the look Mrs. Wilson gave Doug.

"I will take the roll," she repeated. "Carver . . ."

"Here."

"Conrad . . ."

"Here," Jenna squeaked.

"del Rios . . ."

"Here," Miguel answered in the deep, rich voice that had once turned Jenna's knees to jelly.

All of a sudden it was the first day of school again and she was beside herself with the ecstasy of learning that she'd have Miguel del Rios in her homeroom *all year*. Miguel del Rios, the guy she'd crushed on for so long that she'd forgotten other males existed. Jenna couldn't believe their year together was already over.

It went so fast, she thought wistfully. But at the same time, so much had happened. When was the last time she'd even remembered how head-over-heels she'd once been about Miguel?

There's no point remembering it, she thought, blushing. *Even if Miguel wasn't crazy in love with Leah—which he so obviously is—I would never cheat on Peter.*

Still, not that long ago having Miguel flash her one of his smiles would have carried her for a week. Now there wasn't even a week left before his senior activities began.

Then he'll graduate and . . . I'll never sit in a class with him again. The realization hit her like a blast of cold water.

This was the end.

Except not really, she told herself quickly. *Because I'll see him in Eight Prime all summer. And at least he's not moving away next year, like Leah.*

But once he started college, would he still want to hang out with a bunch of high school kids?

"Wallace!" Mrs. Wilson said, finishing the roll

and closing her book with a flourish. "Please take out two pencils, then completely clear your desktops."

"What about the pencils?" someone cracked.

Mrs. Wilson rolled her eyes. "Except for the pencils. Obviously."

In the book-shuffling chaos that ensued, Jenna caught Miguel's eye again. "Good luck," she mouthed, returning his thumbs-up.

I'm going to miss you, she added.

"I just don't know why they have to be so nasty!" Nicole complained, shooting her new squad a furtive look. "I mean what did I ever do to them?"

"Uh-huh," Courtney said absently, not lifting her eyes from her book.

They were eating lunch in the cafeteria that day, except that neither one was eating. Nicole had already pushed her dry salad away, and Courtney's unopened lunch bag lay to one side of her book. Courtney wasn't the only one reading, either. All over the cafeteria, panicky students were trying to memorize texts they'd barely cracked all year, preparing for afternoon finals.

"What test are you studying for?" Nicole asked. Her own two finals that day had been in the morning, and she hadn't sweated them much anyway. So long as she passed—and she knew she had—that was all she cared about.

"Huh?" Courtney finally looked up. "Oh, this isn't for school."

She let Nicole read the cover of her book: *Being, Becoming, Believing!*

"Aren't you getting sick of those yet?" Nicole whined impatiently. "I'm trying to talk to you about something important."

"The other cheerleaders don't accept you," Courtney said, as if such a disaster were a trifle. "I was listening."

"But, Court! What if they never do? It's going to be terrible being on the squad all year with people who don't even like me."

"Wasn't it, like, last week you would have done anything just to get on?" Courtney asked, returning to her book. "Keep being nice and they'll warm up to you sooner or later. What goes around comes around."

"Yeah, right." Nicole chewed her lip with frustration. She wasn't sure which she was more tired of: her best friend's self-help books or her new mantra. She hoped Court was right, of course, but still . . .

I could use a little support here! she thought.

"Reading those books is all you do lately," Nicole accused. "How many have you read, anyway?"

"I've lost count," Courtney admitted, still scanning the words. "Sometimes I read two a day."

"Do they all have such stupid titles?"

Courtney left off reading to glance at the cover again. "They only *seem* stupid until you read the book and find out what they mean."

"Because everything inside is so brilliant," Nicole said sarcastically.

"What's that supposed to mean?" Courtney asked defensively.

"It means come *on*, Court. Some of that stuff you read me . . . well, *Heather* makes more sense than that. You have to admit it's pretty dumb."

Courtney's eyes narrowed dangerously, and for a moment Nicole thought she had finally broken through.

Then her friend took one of those deep, cleansing breaths she'd been practicing lately and fixed Nicole with a pitying smile.

"All right. I'll admit that one or two of the earlier books might have been a bit uninspired in places. But if I hadn't done the psychic work to get to where I am now, how would I know that?"

I know it, and I didn't even read them! Nicole wanted to shout.

Somehow she managed not to say it, picking up her fork to take it out on her salad instead. She stabbed at the hunks of lettuce and sawed a carrot slice, working out her frustration. Satisfied that she had won the argument, Courtney returned to her book.

Psychic work? Nicole thought sullenly. *More like psychobabble.*

She snuck another look at the girls on the cheerleading squad. They continued to pretend to be cramming just so that they could ignore her.

I mean, I understand Court's heart was broken, her world was rocked, et cetera. But does she have to go all weird on me now? Why can't she just go to church like everybody else?

"Pulling a late one, huh?" Leah's father asked, walking into the kitchen to get a glass of water. "How late are you going to stay out here?"

Leah looked up from the physiology notes she'd spread all over the dining room table. "Not much longer. I think I have this stuff down cold."

Her father smiled. "I'm sure you do. You know, Leah, your mom and I are real proud of you."

"I know. You should have seen everyone in the parking lot today, checking out my car. I felt . . . amazing. Like royalty."

"Yeah? I hope you still feel that way when you get to Stanford," he said, leaning against the counter. "A lot of those kids already have more than your mother and I'll ever see. But you know, money isn't everything. These days a happy family seems much more rare than millions." He chuckled. "Try to keep that in mind when your new friends are off skiing, or yachting, or traveling through Europe."

"I know, Dad," she murmured, surprised he thought he needed to say it.

"Besides," he added, a twinkle in his eye, "if you play your cards right, you'll get invited to do that stuff with them."

"So that's your evil plan," Leah teased. "Marry me off to the heir to a winery or something."

"Do wineries make a lot of money?" Mr. Rosenthal asked. "Because I was thinking software tycoon."

"Dad!" Leah exclaimed, throwing her pink eraser at him.

"Speaking of suitors, Shane certainly has his eye on you."

She dropped her eyes to the table, feeling the blush spread up her cheeks.

"He's a good kid," her father added. "I like him."

"You do?" It was completely out of character for Mr. Rosenthal to give any boy a straightforward compliment. Leah waited, anticipating the "but."

Her dad just stood there, drinking his water.

"But . . . ?" she prompted hopefully.

"But nothing. Shane's going to be a star—he's too smart not to be. Not to mention determined. I definitely don't see many students with that type of tenacity."

"Tell me about it," she muttered, her hand straying to the chain at her throat.

"Miguel's a nice kid, but when I look ten years

down the road, I can't begin to guess where he'll be. Shane, on the other hand . . ."

"Will probably be a CEO," Leah admitted past the lump in her throat.

"Exactly." He put the glass down by the sink. "Well, I don't want to keep you up any later than necessary, so I guess I'll say good night. Go to bed soon, all right?"

"I will. I just want to reread a few more pages."

But after he was gone, she found she couldn't concentrate anymore. It *was* late. And she was tired.

And did he have to mention Shane?

Tugging on the chain, she pulled the yin-yang symbol Shane had given her from inside her pajama top. She'd been wearing it under her shirt all day and Miguel hadn't even noticed.

You'd think he would have seen the chain and been at least a little curious, she thought, wondering why she was so annoyed that he hadn't. After all, she hadn't exactly been looking forward to explaining where the necklace had come from. And yet, she hadn't taken it off, either. . . .

Leah sawed the charm back and forth on the chain, thinking about what her father had said. She'd always suspected her dad wasn't Miguel's biggest fan, but she had thought he was warming up to the idea of seeing them as a couple. It hurt to hear him say he thought Shane would go bigger places.

It hurt even more that she couldn't argue with him. Maybe her father was wrong. She hoped so. But from what she knew so far . . .

Shane definitely has the edge on success.

She remembered the way she had leaned up against him the night before. Only for a second. Just long enough to realize how wrong it was. She'd snapped back onto her own feet almost immediately, but there had been that moment. . . .

And she knew he'd felt it too.

I shouldn't have let him get that close. And I never should have let him touch me. I mean, I practically invited the guy to kiss me!

He hadn't, though. He hadn't even tried. And in a way, that bugged her most of all. Shane had never before respected the fact that she was taken. Why now, after she'd practically thrown herself at him?

Maybe I didn't cross the line as far as I thought. I mean, I just leaned on the guy for, like, two seconds. For all he knows, I lost my balance.

She shook her head remorsefully as the double meaning came to her. *I definitely lost my balance.*

The thing was, he *hadn't* kissed her, so everything was fine.

Right?

I just wish I knew why he didn't. I mean, is this some new game he's playing?

Leah got up and paced through the living room, trying to clear her head. The way the whole affair was gnawing at her, it was almost as if she'd *wanted* him to kiss her.

But I didn't, she thought quickly. *I don't.*

Do I?

Ten

Okay. *I'm a member of the squad, and they'll just have to get used to it*, Nicole told herself, screwing up her courage. *It would look bad if I didn't join them, the way they're all sitting together*.

The new cheerleaders had one of the best tables in the cafeteria again that Tuesday, and all of them were there. Tanya, Lou Anne, Angela . . . everyone. Everyone but Nicole.

Fixing that right now, she thought, beginning to walk with her tray.

With finals more than half over, the mood in the cafeteria was more boisterous than the day before. There were still people studying, but most had already either taken their biggest tests or were too burned out to care. Courtney, on the other hand, had finally pulled her nose out of *What Color Is Your Cheese?* and run to the library to cram.

The one exception to every rule.

Nicole's steps slowed as she came within range of the table. She scanned the girls nervously, trying to find the best place to squeeze in. The biggest gap was to one side of Tanya. But if she forced in beside the squad captain, people might think she was trying to make herself look important by association. Kara Tibbs had made room for her before, but this time Kara was wedged between Maria and Sidney with not a whisper of space left between them.

Tanya was always nice to me at Eight Prime events, Nicole reminded herself. In any event, she couldn't keep lollygagging around trying to make up her mind. Taking the final steps forward, she put her tray down next to Tanya's and climbed over the bench between her and Jamila, trying to give the impression that she had some right to be there.

"Hi, Tanya," she said. "How are the fish sticks today?"

Tanya gave her a blank look. "How are they ever?"

"Right. That is so true." Nicole settled into her narrow seat. "I'll probably just eat the Tater Tots."

As if, she added to herself, imagining the fat content. But with the same meal on at least five different trays at the table, it seemed better not to mention caloric excesses. The only reason she'd picked up the hot lunch in the first place was for purposes of blending in.

Nicole ate a green bean, pretending not to notice that conversation at the table had come to a dead halt. *They can't stay quiet forever,* she told herself nervously. *All you have to do is wait them out. . . .*

But after sixty completely silent seconds had gone

130

by, she couldn't take it anymore. She could hear forks clinking, she could hear chewing, she could hear her own heartbeat. And she was desperate to hear something else.

"So. What were you all talking about before I got here?" she finally asked.

Debbie Morris started laughing, and Nicole didn't like the smiles on Lou Anne and Becca's faces either.

"Funny you should ask." Tanya fixed Nicole with deadly serious brown eyes. "We were talking about you."

"Me?" Nicole squeaked. "What about me?"

"Actually, we were talking about how Melanie dropped the squad just so you could take her place."

Nicole felt her lungs squeeze shut. She couldn't breathe at all. She couldn't breathe, she couldn't move . . . she couldn't even think. The reason Melanie had left the squad was supposed to be a secret; no one was ever supposed to find out. But Tanya and Melanie were pretty close, and obviously the cat had clawed its way out of the bag. Maybe Melanie had slipped up somehow, or maybe she'd decided to tell after all.

Either way, the damage was done.

"How, uh—how did you find out?" Nicole asked at last. "Did Melanie say something?"

"*Ha!*" Debbie shrieked triumphantly, pointing at Tanya. "I *told* you! I told you, I told you, I *told* you!"

Angela gave Nicole a disbelieving look, then

131

quickly looked away. All the other girls were staring, the expressions on their faces variously disappointed, disgusted, or just plain mean.

"What did I tell you?" Debbie demanded, looking around the group.

"I don't . . . I don't understand," Nicole stammered.

Tanya shook her head. "Melanie didn't tell me. But you just did. How could you do it, Nicole?"

"Do what? I didn't do anything," she lied desperately. It felt like her brain was being sucked down a pipe, a big swirling funnel of useless gray matter. "I don't even know what you're talking about!"

But it was too late. They'd already read the truth on her face.

"I can't believe we could have had Melanie, and instead we got you," Lou Anne said disgustedly.

"Don't you care about the squad at all?" Sidney asked.

"It wasn't like that!" Nicole protested. "I didn't tell her to do it—she just did! I wish Melanie was still on the squad too."

Becca's light eyes narrowed. "So which of us would you kick off, then?"

"What? No! You're not listen—"

"You could have just said no," Tanya pointed out. "You could have refused to take her place."

"What good would that have done?" There were tears in Nicole's eyes as she pleaded. "You would have just ended up with someone else even further down the cut than me. Besides, I was already on the squad before I found out whose place I was taking. I swear!"

"It's not fair," Debbie said. "We could have had a killer squad."

"We still can!" Nicole insisted. "I mean, I know I'm not Melanie, but—"

"You've got that right," someone muttered.

Nicole's eyes were so full of tears she couldn't even see who had spoken. She picked up a Tater Tot and stuffed it into her mouth—anything not to have to speak. A moment later, though, she knew she had made a mistake. The greasy bits of potato were as dry as ashes in her mouth. She wasn't even sure she'd be able to swallow.

"Just . . . well . . . it's done now," Kara said, addressing the whole table. "Shouldn't we try to get along?"

"It *was* Melanie's decision," Sidney agreed, providing a bit of unexpected aid.

Nicole looked up hopefully.

"We ought to tell Sandra," Lou Anne said. "She's not going to like this one bit."

Nicole felt her lungs collapsing again.

"I'll decide what we tell Sandra," Tanya said sharply. "I don't want this backfiring on Melanie somehow."

"Maybe it should," said Lou Anne. "She deserves it."

"Tanya's the captain," Angela reminded her. "Let her handle this."

"If it weren't for this mess, she'd only be *cocap-tain*," Lou Anne retorted.

Everyone looked at Nicole.

"Sorry," she got out somehow. "I, uh, I really have to study for a final."

Abandoning her barely touched lunch, Nicole picked up her backpack and ran.

They were never going to like her now. She had just sealed her own fate.

I'm such an idiot! she thought, hating herself as the tears streamed down her face. *Why can't I keep my mouth* shut?

Leah walked into her condo Tuesday afternoon and went straight to the answering machine.

"Hooray!" she said at the sight of the blinking red light. Miguel hadn't actually said he would call her, but she'd certainly dropped enough hints. Maybe one had finally penetrated.

She pressed the button.

"Hi, Leah! It's Shane. Give me a call when you get home. My number is 555-2998."

The machine followed up with a long, loud beep. Shane's was the only message on the tape.

"Perfect," Leah muttered, walking to her bedroom.

She had taken Shane's necklace off that morning, feeling like a hypocrite for wearing it as long as she had. If Peter, or Ben, or someone like that had given it to her, she could have worn it without a second thought, safe in the knowledge that it was only a friendly gift. But Shane's friendship came with strings attached, and she couldn't pretend not to know that.

"I can't believe he's calling here now."

Not that she'd done much to discourage him. And her father . . .

Dad probably gave him the number. Although it was in the phone book and the faculty directory. Shane could have gotten it anywhere.

Leah threw her pack onto the bed and plopped down beside it. *Should I call him? Should I ignore him?*

Ignoring a problem wasn't her style. If she tried, she knew it would eat her up, and she didn't want any more on her mind with CCHS's last finals the next day. On the other hand, she didn't want to encourage Shane, either. It wasn't as if she were going to make a habit of calling him, or calling him back— or having anything to do with him, for that matter.

"That's what I ought to tell him. I'll call him and tell him that."

Getting off the bed, Leah walked back out to the answering machine on the kitchen counter. Her parents still weren't home from work, so now was the perfect time to set Shane straight. She played back his message and copied the number, then completely erased the tape.

I'm going to tell him he's pushing too hard, and that if

he wants to stay friends, he needs to back off. I'll see him when we get to California, and that's that, she decided, dialing the phone.

A guy picked up on the third ring.

"Hi," she said hesitantly. "Is, uh, Shane there?"

The phone clunked down on something hard. "*Shaa*-aane!" the voice yelled in mocking singsong. "It's one of your little *girl*friends."

Leah felt her resolve stiffen.

"Hi, this is Shane," he said, picking up the telephone.

"It's Leah," she said tensely.

"Leah! Finally! I was starting to think you were ignoring me. Which wouldn't be very nice, by the way. What time do you get home from school?"

"I stayed late to study for a final. I just got home."

"Oh, well. That explains it," he said happily.

"But even if I'd gotten home earlier, I can't always drop everything just to return phone calls," she added, not liking him to sound so relieved. "Honestly, I don't think you should be calling me anyway."

"Ooh. Someone's in a bad mood. Finals stressing you out?"

"A lot of things are stressing me out." She left it to him to fill in the blanks.

"My last week of high school was a blast," he said obliviously. "I mean, so you take a few tests. So what? After that it's just fun, fun, fun. Where's the senior picnic this year?"

This conversation obviously was going to take longer than she'd hoped. Leah sighed and sat on a barstool. "The lake. It's *always* at the lake."

"Are you driving the new car?"

"Probably." A horrible premonition struck her. "But don't you dare come looking for me. I'm going to be busy. And besides, I don't think they'll let you in."

Shane laughed. "Don't worry. I'm not *that* nostalgic for high school. Besides, I think I'm a little old for senior picnics. Don't you?"

"You're too old for senior picnics but not too old for me?" she challenged.

"Like I said before, you're different. It's not like I *need* to chase high school girls. There are plenty of interested parties right here."

"So I hear," she said sourly, remembering the way Shane's roommate had answered the phone.

He laughed again. "Can I help it if I'm popular?" His voice turned sly. "You're not jealous, are you?"

"No!" she said, wishing too late she had sounded less sulky. If she didn't care, why was she getting so bent out of shape?

"Good. Because I know you're so true to Miguel."

Was he making fun of her?

"That's right," she said.

"For now."

"Forever!"

"Nothing's forever, Leah. You've been around long enough to know that, I'm sure."

"Look, Shane, I'm not going to talk to you if that's how you're going to be. If you can't respect the fact that I have a boyfriend, then I think you'd better just stay away from—"

"All right, all right! Don't get so hot! I was just teasing. You take everything so seriously."

Leah exhaled slowly. "Family trait," she admitted.

"Well, that's not a bad thing. Necessarily. But you have to have fun sometimes too, right?"

"I think the problem hinges on your definition of fun."

"Fair enough. What do *you* think is fun?"

"I don't know. Hanging out. Reading."

"Yeah? Have you read that new thriller about the guy who clones killer sharks? Man, I'm glad I don't live by the beach." Some of the usual glee crept back into his voice. "Yet."

"I mostly read nonfiction."

"Like what? Not textbooks!"

"I do enjoy scholarly works," Leah said, a little primly. "I also read a lot of biographies, history, religion—"

"Philosophy," he cut her off.

She smiled into the receiver. "Right."

"So what do you think about God? Or do you think about God?"

"All the time. That's one of life's big questions. Isn't it?"

"Maybe. What are the other questions?"

She started to answer, then laughed. "What are you doing?"

"Me?" he said innocently. "I'm just trying to have a conversation with my *friend* Leah. Nothing wrong with that, is there?"

"Depends on your motives."

"What motives?" he protested. "Why do there have to be motives?"

"Because there always are, Shane. You've been around long enough to know that, I'm sure."

"Oh. You're good," he said, chuckling as he registered her hit. "You are very good indeed."

Maybe he was flirting, maybe he wasn't. He probably was. But it felt good to match wits with someone on her level. Challenging, exciting, maybe even a little dangerous . . .

I made my position clear. He knows this is all just talk.

"I *am* good," she replied smugly, leaning back on her stool.

I can handle Shane.

Melanie was racing through the Book of Matthew in the study Bible Peter had loaned her when she thought she heard a noise on the stairs. She froze, waiting to hear if her father was coming up from the den.

Don't come in here, she willed silently, staring at her closed bedroom door.

She had just started rereading the New Testament, and it was actually making sense this time. The English in Peter's study version was much easier to understand than in her mother's old Bible; plus it was almost as if someone were reading her mind, with all the questions and answers typed in the margins. Nearly every question she thought of was already written out right there, along with an explanation. She even understood what the begats were all about now.

There was no further sound from outside her room. Relaxing back into her pillows, she started reading again.

A single light knock made her snap bolt upright just as her father cracked open her bedroom door and stuck his head inside.

"Dad!" she protested, closing the Bible over her thumb and pressing its cover down into her lap. "I didn't say come in!"

"Oops. Sorry. I thought you fell asleep with the light on, and I was just going to turn it out."

"It's not that late, is it?" she asked, checking the clock on her nightstand: nearly midnight. "Oh. A little later than I realized," she admitted.

"Hitting the books, huh?" he said, leaning against her doorway. He was wearing his favorite ratty bathrobe and slippers, but despite the amount of time he'd spent hanging out in the den that night, he didn't seem too intoxicated. "What are you studying?"

"Nothing. Just reading." She pushed the Bible deeper into her lap, trying to hide it.

"Reading what?"

Melanie worked to keep her face impassive. "A book Peter lent me."

"It's thick enough. What's the title?"

The one time he takes some interest in what I'm doing . . . , she thought, wondering if she could get away with making something up. *But what if he asks to see it? And anyway, why should I lie? I'm not doing anything wrong.*

Reluctantly raising the book, Melanie let him read the cover for himself.

"The Bible!" he exclaimed, floored. "Peter thinks you have nothing better to do than read the *Bible?*"

"I wanted to read it."

"What for?" His question was partly just the attitude she'd expected, but she could tell another part was genuine. He truly didn't understand. "You've never read it? Not in your whole life?"

"I don't know. Maybe parts. When I was a kid."

"Well, there you go. I just want to see what it says. What it *really* says, I mean. Not what people say it says."

He rolled his eyes. "I sure don't see the attraction. Besides, why are you wasting time with that now, during finals?"

"If I thought I was wasting time, I wouldn't do it," she said testily.

141

He opened his mouth to argue, then shrugged it off. "I guess it's of some use. From a historical perspective, I mean. Most of our laws are based on it." He smiled as a second thought occurred to him. "And it could be a big help if you ever go on *Jeopardy*!"

"I'm not reading it for trivia."

"Then why?"

"I just . . . What if it's true? Do you ever think about that?"

Mr. Andrews shook his head. "You've been hanging around those Christian kids too long. I hope this isn't about being afraid of going to hell again."

When she was younger that had happened a couple of times—so-called friends attempting to convert her by scaring her to death. Once she had even come home crying. But her heart had long since hardened to those types of threats, and to the people who made them.

"Not at all," she said. "I'm afraid of missing the point."

"What point?"

"Exactly! If there *is* a point to all this—being alive, being here—wouldn't you like to know what it is?"

He shook his head again, a little wearily. "And you think you're going to find it in the Bible."

It seems at least as likely as you finding it in a six-pack, she thought, wishing she had the guts to say it.

"I'm just reading. That's all."

"It's your brain," he said, retreating. "But don't stay up much later," he added, pulling her door closed behind him.

Melanie's heart continued to pound for a long time after he'd gone. Still, she was proud of the way she'd stood up for herself. She had spoken her mind—mostly—and for once she hadn't let him force his depressing views on her. Not only that, but now that he knew she was reading the Bible, she didn't have to hide it anymore.

The prospect was incredibly freeing. Whether the Bible was right or wrong, it felt fantastic simply to assert her right to read it. After all, why *shouldn't* she read it?

I'm practically an adult now. I'll make my own decisions.

Eleven

"So how was water safety class?" Mrs. Brewster asked when Nicole arrived home on Wednesday.

Nicole groaned and dropped her wet stuff in the entry. "Don't ask. Ben gave himself a rope burn with the rescue tube and almost pulled my top off in the process."

Her mother scowled. "I told you to wear a one-piece."

"I know," Nicole admitted, "but no one saw anything. Besides, I'm definitely not being rescued by Ben again. I'd rather drown."

Walking into the house, she checked her reflection in the antique entryway mirror. All her makeup had washed off, even though she had just invested a big chunk of allowance in new, supposedly waterproof stuff. Her blond hair hung to her shoulders in damp, swampy-smelling strings.

"One thing I can tell you," she added grouchily. "Once we get these stupid certificates, somebody *will* have to be drowning before I put my head back under that lake."

Mrs. Brewster chuckled. "I don't like to get my hair wet either."

"Wet hair is the tip of the *Titanic* iceberg," Nicole said, pulling herself away from the mirror. "The whole class is such a pain. Ken acts like we'll be dragging bodies up off the bottom every day, Peter runs around like our mother or something, and Jenna . . . I don't know *what's* gotten into Jenna. I said I might be a little late to the last class on Saturday, and I thought she'd pop a vein. I mean, people have lives, after all—or at least they're supposed to. I don't know why I should get up at dawn on the very first day of vacation."

"It won't kill you. How'd you do on your history test?"

"Fine. I think." The essay question at the end had come out of nowhere, but other than that she felt pretty secure. "At least finals are over!"

"So how are they going to keep you all busy at school the next two days?" Mrs. Brewster asked.

"The seniors have their picnic tomorrow, and rehearsal on Friday. The rest of us will just be signing yearbooks and killing time. I predict a lot of boring films." Nicole brightened with a new idea. "Maybe they'll give up and just let us go early. Wouldn't that be great?"

"Yeah. Dream on," said her mother, waving her toward the stairs. "If you hurry, you still have time to shower before dinner. And don't leave wet stuff by the door!" she added as she headed back into the kitchen.

Nicole picked up her towel and backpack and dragged them up the stairs to her room, still thinking about the last days of school. No matter what a waste they were, at least there were only two left. And water safety class only had one more session. She could survive anything for that long, and after that it was summer: sleeping in, lying out, and, of course, cheerleading camp.

Not that she was looking forward to camp anymore. Melanie had taken the news of Nicole's blunder surprisingly well, but all day long at school Nicole had lain as low as she could anyway, terrified that Sandra would come looking for her about it. That hadn't happened, so she could only assume that Tanya hadn't told. Even so, wasn't the news bound to get back to the coach sometime? And what would happen then? Just thinking about the possibilities gave Nicole a knot in her belly the size of an eight ball.

I just have to become the best girl on the squad. The best in the whole camp. If I really knock them dead—

The phone rang, startling her out of her thoughts. Nicole walked into the bathroom she shared with her sister and put her head through the doorway on the other side, checking Heather's room. The little monster wasn't there, but Nicole closed her door anyway before she lifted the cordless phone out of its cradle.

"Hello?"

"Nicole? It's Guy."

"Hi, Guy," she said, hoping to sound casual but feeling kind of nervous just the same. She hadn't spoken to him once since their not-so-great date at the salad bar.

"What have you been doing?" he asked.

For a second, she felt like telling him everything— how messed up things were with the squad and how stressed out she was about it. She knew he could be a good listener, and there was nobody else that she wanted to confide in. Given his opinions on cheerleading, though, it didn't seem smart to mention how much the other girls hated her. He'd just tell her to drop the squad.

"Nothing," she said at last.

"Are your finals over?"

"Yeah. How about yours?" Ozarks Prep, the Christian private school Guy attended, didn't always keep the same schedule as CCHS.

"I have my last one tomorrow, then Friday is Ditch Day."

"Ditch Day?" she repeated doubtfully. Sanctioned ditching sounded far too liberal for such a conservative school.

"I don't know why they call it that," he admitted.

"Everyone still has to come, but all the classrooms are open and we just wander around and sign yearbooks. There's a barbecue for lunch. Then, in the afternoon, the seniors graduate and everyone goes to see that."

"Oh." It sounded all right, if less grandiose than the three days of senior activities at CCHS. "I guess your school is pretty small."

"Yeah, but we have a good time. Our year-end dance is Saturday night. Want to go?"

The suddenness of his invitation took her by surprise.

"Well, um, is it formal?" she asked. He had already seen her one acceptable dress—and her mother had already vetoed buying her another.

"Not at all. I mean, some people will dress up a little, but it's supposed to be casual. The whole school goes, and we have a live band—you can wear jeans if you want."

"I see," she said absently, mentally running through potential outfits. She could still fit into her skinniest U.S. Girls jeans, but those wouldn't make her stand out much in a crowd.

Maybe I should go for something more sophisticated. My green dress is cute, or I could borrow something of Courtney's. Ooh! I wonder if she'd let me wear her black leather—

"So do you want to go?" Guy asked.

"What? Oh. Sure."

"Should I pick you up at six-thirty?" he asked. "We can get some dinner beforehand."

"Okay. No, wait!" she cried, remembering. "Our graduation is that night, and I definitely want to go. What time does the dance start?"

"Eight."

Nicole did some quick calculations. The CCHS graduation ceremony started at six. If it lasted an hour and a half, and it took her fifteen minutes to get home . . .

Then my makeup will be at least two hours old. Besides, I don't want to wear the same outfit both places.

"How about picking me up at my house at eight?" she asked. "Sorry about dinner, but I really want to see my friends graduate, and we shouldn't be *too* late to the dance that way."

"No problem," he agreed. "Eight it is."

Nicole got off the phone and went straight to her closet, totally forgetting that she was supposed to be taking a shower.

"Pants or a dress?" she wondered aloud.

She clicked through the hangers on one side of the closet, then the other, waiting for something to catch her eye. In a lot of ways, dressing casual was trickier than dressing up. It was no easy thing to turn heads without looking like that was the goal.

Oh, well. If we have as much fun as we did at the prom, I don't really care what I wear. Much.

She closed her eyes and pictured her romantic moment with Guy at the prom, the one where he'd been about to kiss her. If Courtney hadn't chosen that exact moment to break things up, who knew how different things might be between them right now? That kiss could have changed everything.

Nicole sighed, then opened her eyes and pulled a slinky silk blouse from the closet.

This could be our chance to pick up where we left off.

"Well, what do you want to do now?" Leah asked.

Miguel shrugged, jostling the picked-over paper plate in his lap. "There's nothing much *to* do, is there? At least here we have seats in the shade."

Leah set her own plate aside on the small patch of grass she and Miguel had staked out, downhill from the main parking lot. Far away down the slope, at the lakeshore, the grills were still turning out seconds and thirds on hamburgers, and the grisly remains of thirty watermelons lay strewn across a picnic table, dripping seedless gore through the boards to the sand. CCHS seniors swarmed up and down the shore like ants, the girls in tank tops or sundresses, the guys running around with their T-shirts hanging out of their back pockets. A few lucky people had staked out rocks or benches to sit on; even fewer had brought beach chairs, setting them up in groups at the water's edge. Most milled about on the wide stretch of sand or waded with the mud squishing up through their toes, talking, laughing, and just being sociable.

"We should go down there," Leah said.

Miguel made a face. "Someone will take our spot."

"Does it matter? We're done eating."

The only reason she had agreed to move so far out of the action in the first place was because Miguel had insisted he needed to sit down to eat. With one hand balancing a loaded plate and the other holding a freezing cold soda, she had seen the sense of his argument. But lunch was over now—and she was starting to feel like they were missing all the fun.

Miguel surveyed the scene below them with a totally bored expression. "There's nothing going on down there. I'd rather stay where I am."

"What about what *I'd* rather do?"

He shrugged again. "Go, if you want. I'll wait here."

"I don't think you're getting it," she said, working hard to keep her voice pleasant. "See, here we are—seniors, at last—and this is our senior picnic. We shouldn't be sitting up here while it passes us by, we should be down there talking to people. As a *couple*," she added when Miguel still didn't move.

"Who, exactly, do you want to talk to?"

She didn't appreciate his jaded tone, but she had to admit he had a point. They knew other people separately, but as a couple they almost never hung out with anyone besides Eight Prime. And since no one else in Eight Prime was a senior . . .

"There's Mindy Patterson and some girls from my P.E. class," she said, pointing down to the water's edge. The girls were giggling in a tight little group, casting repeated glances at some guys kicking water at each other.

"Gee, that looks like fun. I can't wait."

"Then who do *you* want to talk to?" she demanded. "Let's hear *your* suggestion."

"I don't know. If we really have to do this, I guess we could go bug Mike and Roger."

He pointed down the shore, at a gang composed entirely of guys trying to outdo each other in feats of machismo. Some of them had water guns; others, water balloons. Roger and Mike, Miguel's old water polo buddies, had mud smeared across their bare chests and streaked on their faces like war paint.

Pass, Leah thought immediately. She wasn't in the mood to model a wet T-shirt.

"Well, they're going to start the games pretty soon," she said. "What about the egg toss? Let's go down and sign up for that."

"Are you serious?"

"Why not?"

"Because the *best* thing that can happen in an egg toss is that you crush a raw egg in your hands.

More likely, it ends up on your shirt. Or someone else throws theirs at you on purpose, just to get a laugh."

"Well, we have to do something!" she said, just barely hanging on to her temper. "Why are you acting this way?"

"I'm *tired*, Leah. And I have a million other things on my mind. I don't know why we can't just sit here on the grass and relax."

"What do you have on your mind?" she demanded. "Finals are over, graduation's not until Saturday, and today is supposed to be fun."

"You think school's all I think about?" he asked incredulously. "Just the opposite. I hardly think about school at all."

"What, then?"

"Everything! Life, and the hospital, and my mom, and Rosa . . . moving us into a place of our own. I'm thinking of going over to Charlie's this week and asking him how much he wants for that house."

Leah sighed, exasperated. "Why do you torture yourself? Whatever he wants, you know you don't have it."

"I don't have it *yet*," he corrected. "But if Charlie's not in a hurry, and if I go back to work in construction for Mr. Ambrosi . . ."

Leah shook her head. "Wake up, Miguel! We're

graduating here, and you're more interested in that stupid house!"

"So what if I am?" he asked, bristling. "What's wrong with wanting a house?"

"There's nothing wrong with it, but you're obsessive! I mean, look at us right now. This is our senior picnic. We ought to be down there soaking up every last minute of high school together . . . because no matter what we think is going to happen, who can honestly say where you and I will be this time next year? This is it, Miguel—this is the end of high school—and I feel like you're cheating me out of it. If you're planning to be this much dead weight on grad night, tell me now and I'll go to the amusement park with someone else."

Shane flashed into her mind, uninvited. She had meant she'd hang out with some girlfriends. Still, it was impossible to imagine Shane ignoring her like Miguel was . . .

"Well, excuse me," Miguel returned. "But you're the one who dragged me to this stupid thing in the first place. And as far as Charlie's house goes, that's real life, Leah. That's *my* life. How can you even compare it to something as lame as high school?"

"Are you saying doing things with me isn't real life?" she asked, furious.

"Of course not. Don't be so—"

But Leah didn't wait to hear what he thought she was being. Jumping to her feet, she took long strides

154

toward the crowd on the sand, brushing grass off her shorts as she went.

"Leah!" he called after her.

"Enjoy your *shade*!" she shot back, barely turning her head.

If Miguel didn't appreciate her company, she'd find somebody who did.

Twelve

The last day of school, Melanie thought, walking across CCHS's lush front lawn toward the main building. *Hallelujah!*

She could hardly wait for the final bell to ring so that she could stop hiding from all the people she'd been avoiding the last few days. Steve, for one, but also the cheerleading squad, and especially the cheerleading coach. Ever since Tuesday night, when Nicole had called to admit that she'd accidentally spilled the beans about Melanie's real reason for leaving the squad, Melanie had been living in fear of some sort of confrontation.

Well, I'm almost home free now, she thought, losing herself in the horde of students swarming onto campus.

A person could tell just by looking around that it was the last day. Everyone was pushing the fashion envelope, wearing outfits that would qualify as borderline demerit material the rest of the year. The sandals were strappier, and so were the tops; shorts were hemmed absurdly high or slung equally low, depending on which sex was wearing them; and the girls in their pastel sundresses looked like flocks of long-legged butterflies. Melanie smiled as she walked up the entrance steps with the crowd pouring into the building. There was something cheerful about the atmosphere that day, a sense of thankfulness and relief so palpable she imagined she could smell it drifting through the hall like a summer breeze.

She made it all the way to her locker with the smile still on her face before Tanya knocked it off.

"Cleaning out your locker?" Tanya asked, sneaking up with Angela. "Are you sure you wouldn't rather have *Nicole* do that for you?"

Melanie winced. "Yeah, right. Very funny."

"How could you do it, Melanie?" Angela asked, a bit plaintively. "That's what no one understands. I know she's your friend and all, but did you ever stop to think how the rest of us would feel? I mean, aren't we your friends too?"

"Of course," Melanie said uncomfortably, pretending to look for something at the back of her locker. "You know it's not like that."

"You could at least have *told* us," Tanya said. "It sucks that we had to find out the way we did."

"I know," Melanie admitted. "I just thought it was better to keep secret. After all, it doesn't really matter why I left. And I thought things would be smoother for Nicole if people believed she got in on her own."

"So much for that idea!" Tanya snorted. "Even the new girls know we'd be much better off with you."

"No, you *don't* know that." Melanie glanced worriedly around the crowded hallway, but between the slamming lockers and excited last-day greetings, there was little chance of anyone overhearing their conversation. "Has, uh, Sandra said anything?" she asked, her heart up in her throat.

"No, because I don't think she knows," said Angela. "If she does, she didn't hear it from us."

Melanie breathed a sigh of relief. "Well, that's something. She seemed kind of mad at me for dropping, and I'd hate for her to take it out on Nicole."

"Don't worry," Tanya said. "The squad's got that covered without Sandra."

"What do you mean?" Melanie asked apprehensively.

"Nobody likes her," Tanya said bluntly.

"Why not?"

"It's not that there's anything *wrong* with her," Angela said, shifting back and forth on her heels. "She's just not . . . you."

"She doesn't fit in," Tanya said.

"You have to give her a chance!" Nicole hadn't mentioned any of this to Melanie. *Does she even realize there's a problem?*

Angela nodded slightly, setting her long curls

bobbing. "I'm sure it would be different if you and she were both on the squad. She's—"

"Well, I'm *not* on the squad. But you guys are. And if you're really my friends, you'll look out for Nicole."

"Don't put this on me," Tanya said with a groan.

"No, I mean it," Melanie insisted. "I gave up a lot. Don't make it be for nothing."

She stared them both down determinedly, until tenderhearted Angela finally caved.

"We'll be nice to her," she promised. "We can start at the squad meeting this afternoon."

Tanya still didn't seem convinced. "Maybe if you just talk to Sandra . . . ," she began.

"No! Nobody's talking to Sandra," Melanie said quickly. "What's done is done. You'll just have to make it work."

"If you're sure that's what you want," said Angela.

"It is. Really, you guys. Nicole can take some getting used to, but she's okay once you get to know her. Give her a chance and you'll like her, I swear."

Tanya rolled her eyes, a hint of an embarrassed smile on her face. "I guess."

Melanie hugged both her friends gratefully. "You will," she promised. "You'll see."

"Now listen up!" Principal Kelly bellowed through his megaphone to the crowd standing on the grass. "You see those letters up there?"

From his perch on the specially erected graduation bleachers, he pointed across the football field into the permanent stands, where twenty-six widely spaced students were holding signs over their heads. "All you seniors, split up and go sit down according to the first letter of your last name."

There were groans throughout the crowd. Leah's hand tightened on Miguel's.

"Why can't we stay with our friends?" someone shouted, voicing Leah's thoughts exactly. "Why does it have to be alphabetical?"

"Because I have to read all your names," Principal Kelly explained reasonably, "which means I have to have a list, and the school's official list of students is alphabetical. If I let you all come up and tell me what order you're going to walk in, we'll still be here when football starts."

There were a few laughs, and a few more groans, as the crowd reluctantly began to comply.

"I wanted to walk with you," Miguel said.

"Me too. With you, I mean," Leah murmured, blinking back tears. She had known it probably wouldn't be possible, but she had let herself hope just the same. She and Miguel had missed most of the picnic arguing with each other, and even though they had made up before the end, they couldn't replace the time they had wasted. She had hoped commencement rehearsal would be different.

"We could cut out of here," he suggested. "We could go hang out somewhere else and just fake it tomorrow."

"We can't. My parents are coming to watch, and so's your mom. I don't want to look stupid, do you?"

Miguel shrugged. "They've already printed the diplomas. It's not like they're going to flunk us for marching out of step."

"Come on, people. Get a move on!" the principal shouted through his megaphone.

Leah looked from the D's at one end of the bleachers to the R's way at the other. She and Miguel weren't even going to be able to see each other.

"As soon as this is over, then let's go somewhere," she said. "It's Friday, and we don't have to be home until late. I'll just call my parents and—"

"Can't," Miguel said. "I'm working tonight."

"Tonight?" she repeated, unable to believe her ears. "I asked you yesterday and you said you weren't!"

The face he made proved he had known she'd be mad. "I wasn't going to, but then Mr. Ambrosi called and said he had a bunch of people out sick and—"

"*He* called *you*? Or you called him?" Leah asked suspiciously.

Miguel had been talking about going back to work for his former boss ever since he had quit. She hated the idea that he would leave such a good opportunity at the hospital just to return to construction. More than that, she hated the idea of her boyfriend work-ing side by side again with the boss's daughter, gor-geous and overly friendly Sabrina Ambrosi.

"He called me. I swear," said Miguel. "He's got a big painting project this weekend, and—"

"If you work this weekend, I'll break up with you," she said, surprising them both. Even so, she didn't take it back. "I mean it. Working during graduation is like working during your honeymoon. There are just certain times—"

"I'm not working this weekend, all right? I already told him he's on his own after tonight. But I couldn't just say no, because I want some hours this summer. A lot of hours, I hope. That's good money, Leah."

It was always about money with Miguel. Leah had to bite her lip not to say so. She knew he was only trying to help his family, but did he *always* have to put her after work, after his mother and sister, even after Charlie's stupid house?

"Ms. Rosenthal," the principal's voice boomed. "If you could kindly tear yourself away from your boyfriend and take your seat, maybe we could get started."

Leah cringed and started walking, ignoring the titters from the stands. Knowing the principal per-sonally had its drawbacks, but a bit of teasing was nothing compared to the deeper truth of his words.

She felt like she *was* tearing herself away from her

boyfriend—or that Miguel was tearing himself away from her. All around her, people were psyched about graduating, laughing and living it up like they didn't have a care in the world, but Leah wished she could turn back the clock. She still wanted to go to Stanford, to see the world outside Clearwater Crossing, but she was finally starting to appreciate how much she'd be leaving behind.

You knew this day would come, she reminded herself as she climbed the bleachers to join the other R's. *You knew when you decided not to marry Miguel that he wouldn't follow you to California.*

But it wasn't just Miguel, she realized now, fighting off fresh tears. It was everything, and everyone: all her other friends at school, Eight Prime, the familiar old buildings themselves. She had been happy at CCHS—and now she was leaving it for good. Soon she'd be leaving her home, her hometown, her parents. . . .

Even when she came back to visit, things could never be the same. It would all be different because *she'd* be different.

And the changes were starting already.

Taking a seat on the edge of her group, Leah felt a tear slide down her cheek. She brushed it away with one hand, fishing for her dark glasses and putting them on with the other. The sun was pounding the bleachers that morning, but Leah had an even better reason for hiding her eyes. She felt a sudden kinship with all the other students in sunglasses, wondering how many of them were secretly crying too.

I'm going to miss this place, she realized, trying to sear its memory into her brain. She studied the shape of the football field and the jagged rooftops of the buildings beyond. After she had gone, she wanted to be able to close her eyes and picture the trees fringing the parking lot, to smell the steamy new-mown grass, even to feel the heat of the bench warming the backs of her thighs. She wanted to see all these same people, to recall the life lessons she had learned the hard way . . . to always stay who she was right then, at that exact moment in time.

I'm going to miss high school more than I ever guessed.

Maybe I should just give them what they want and drop out, Nicole thought, shuffling unhappily down the hall toward the final cheerleading meeting of the year.

School had just been dismissed for the summer, and all around her people were going crazy—slamming lockers, shouting unrepeatable farewells, and literally bouncing off the walls with the joy of three months' vacation. Trash was everywhere underfoot, ankle-deep in some places and getting deeper as procrastinators now emptied their lockers directly onto the floor in their hurry to be gone. Nicole had cleaned her own locker out at noon, returning her books and dumping her garbage. All that remained were the few things she carried in her backpack and the deposit check for cheerleading camp she now held in her hands.

I don't even want to go, she thought numbly. It seemed impossible that she could think that way after everything she'd endured just to get the opportunity, but that was how she felt.

Why should I go? Nobody likes me.

For a moment she actually considered turning tail and sprinting for the parking lot. Courtney was waiting for her out there, so engrossed in *Six Steps to Selfhood* that she hadn't even objected to hanging around in ninety-degree heat. Nicole stopped walking and leaned against a wall, barely aware of the chaos around her.

Maybe I should have told Melanie how mean they are to me. Maybe she could have helped.

A second later she shook her head. *No, I was right not to say anything. She's already given me everything. I can't go crying to Melanie every time I have a problem, like some pathetic little baby.*

Even so, she could no longer deny that there was a large and growing part of her that wished she could give Melanie's gift back. When Melanie had been on the squad, everyone had been happy except Nicole. Now everyone was miserable, including Nicole. If she had simply accepted the fact that she wasn't good enough, never had been good enough, never would be good enough . . .

Stop feeling sorry for yourself! she thought, beginning to walk again. *You wanted to be a cheerleader, and now you are. For Pete's sake, suck it up.*

After all, it wasn't as if the girls were going to say anything to her in front of Sandra. She didn't think.

And you don't need to say anything either. Just go along with whatever the group decides about camp and keep your big mouth shut. Sit in a chair, hand over your check, and keep your big mouth shut. You ought to be able to handle that.

Even so, she wasn't sorry to see that Sandra had beat her to the classroom where the meeting was being held. Nicole was the last one there.

"You're late, Nicole," said Sandra, glancing at the clock. It was barely two minutes past the meeting time.

"I'm sorry. I was—"

"Never mind," the coach said abruptly. "Let's get this show on the road. Did everyone bring their checks?"

Unanimous answers of "yes" and "I did" greeted the coach's question.

"Good, then sit down and let's wrap this up."

There was a line of chairs facing the front of the room, and the girls began pulling them into a circle. Nicole picked up a chair for herself, then froze, wondering where she was going to put it.

"Here, Nicole," Angela called unexpectedly. "We have some room over here."

Quickly, before she could wake up and discovered she'd dreamed it, Nicole set her chair down where Angela pointed, in the space right between her and Tanya.

"Thanks," she murmured gratefully.

Angela shrugged. "No problem."

And was Tanya actually smiling at her? Nicole flashed a sickly smile in return, then sat down fast, feeling the need for something solid beneath her.

"All right," Sandra said, addressing the whole squad. "I've talked this over with Tanya, and from what she tells me I gather the group is leaning toward Camp Twist-n-Shout. Is that what you've all agreed on?"

No one had ever asked Nicole where she wanted to go, but she'd memorized the brochures, and Camp Twist-n-Shout had looked good to her. Not that she'd have dared to speak up even if she had hated it . . .

"I didn't think anything had been decided for certain yet," Debbie said. "They put more emphasis on stunts at Camp Pride, so I think we'd be better off there."

"We don't do that many stunts," Tanya said.

"That's because we don't know any," said Lou Anne. "I like Camp Pride too."

Sandra sighed. Things weren't as settled as she'd obviously thought.

"Not to influence your decision," she said, "but you might want to keep in mind that stunts are only a small part of a squad's repertoire. Camp Twist-n-Shout offers stunts too, so maybe you ought to focus on who has the best cheer and dance programs."

"We already know how to cheer and dance," Debbie said stubbornly. "And we'll only be at camp four days. Why not learn what we can't get here?"

"I'm not completely unfamiliar with stunts," Sandra said stiffly. "Principal Kelly is the one who put them off limits, and we still don't know for certain that they'll be cleared for next year."

"We don't want to spend all our time learning stuff we might not even be able to use," Angela said. "Besides, Camp Twist-n-Shout has a stunt clinic too. I vote for Camp Twist-n-Shout."

"Good idea," said Sandra. "Let's take a vote. Majority wins. Fair enough?"

Heads nodded nervously. The room became very quiet.

"All right, then. Who votes for Camp Twist-n-Shout?"

Five hands went into the air: Tanya's, Angela's, Kara's, Maria's, and Becca's. A tie. Nicole sat paralyzed, wondering what she should do. She didn't want to vote; she didn't even care. And no matter how she picked, she'd be voting against somebody.

Then a slight movement from Tanya caught her attention. The cocaptain's brown eyes were intense as she looked meaningfully from Nicole's face to the hands resting in Nicole's lap, then up into the air.

168

There was no mistaking the squad leader's message. Holding her breath, half closing her eyes, Nicole slowly raised her hand. Six to four.

Except that then something interesting happened.

"Yeah, me too," Sidney said quickly. Her hand shot into the air, in perfect sync with Jamila's.

Eight to two.

Nicole had chosen right! Not only had she shown her loyalty to Tanya, she'd aligned herself with the vast majority of the squad. She barely even cared that she'd voted against Debbie and Lou Anne. Those two were the meanest anyway, and if she only ever won over the other seven, she could live with that.

"All right. Camp Twist-n-Shout it is," Sandra said. "Please fill in that name on the payee part of your checks, then pass them in to me."

People started digging for pens. Nicole took the opportunity to sneak another look at Tanya.

To her surprise, the captain smiled at her again, a conspirator's grin this time. Casting a look to her other side, Nicole found Angela grinning as well.

I'm in! she realized gleefully, scrawling "Camp Twist-n-Shout" across her mother's check.

She still wasn't sure why Angela had invited her to sit with them in the first place, but voting for the camp they wanted had definitely sealed the deal. They accepted her now, or at least they'd decided to give her a chance. And if Tanya and Angela came out in her favor, who would dare to give her grief?

Now I can make the rest of them like me. I just need to have a plan!

Handing her check to Sandra, Nicole took a small spiral notepad out of her backpack. She thought for a second, then began writing as fast as she could.

Things to take to camp:
  5 workout outfits ~ cute.
  5 regular outfits ~ even cuter
     (borrow Court's green T-top!)
Extra shorts & tops to loan
Sweats?
Make Mom buy me those cool
     pj's at the mall
Makeup- bring it ALL!
Scrunchies, gel, & hair stuff
     (pack separate kit?)
Herbal Extravagance shampoo
Blow dryer, curling iron
Crimper?
Cheer! & Modern Girl mags.
Snacks
lots of snacks
Snacks for everyone!!

Thirteen

"This is the last drill, so pay attention and we'll all get out of here early!" Ken shouted from the shore.

Jenna smiled and wriggled her toes on the muddy lake bottom. All of Eight Prime was out there with her, standing in waist-deep water, and for once they were working together as a tight, efficient team. Every drill so far that morning had been perfect—or close enough to satisfy her rapidly relaxing standards.

Maybe people really were *just distracted by school and finals and all*, she thought. Whatever the problem had been, it seemed behind them now, and Jenna's spirits rose by the second. *I can't believe it's the first day of summer!*

Forget what the calendar said; as far as Jenna was concerned summer always began on the first day of vacation and ended on the first day of school. Three whole months stretched before her now, full of sunshine and promise.

"Okay, here's the scenario," Ken told them. "All the campers are swimming. You've just done your regular buddy check, and you find out you have a kid missing. His buddy was fooling around, looking for frogs in the reeds, and now he has no idea where this kid is. What do you do?"

"Panic," Jenna murmured, shivering at the possibility.

"No lie," Melanie whispered behind her.

"You have to assume he's in the water," Miguel answered.

"Right," said Ken. "For all you know, he just took off to use the john, but work from the worst-case scenario backward. If he *is* in the water, you don't want to waste time checking the bathroom before you start searching the lake."

"You could send one person to go look in the bathroom, and the cabin, and anyplace else they can think of while everyone else checks the lake," Peter said.

"Who's watching the other kids?" Nicole asked.

"Excellent point," Ken said.

Nicole beamed and adjusted the straps of her miniature red bikini.

"The first thing we ought to do is get all the kids out of the water," said Jesse. "Get them out and make them sit down somewhere so it only takes one person to watch them."

Ken nodded. "Exactly. You need to have a procedure, and you need to drill it with the kids. When you blow the whistle a certain way, they all come straight out and sit by that tree, for example," he said pointing. "Or maybe under the flagpole. You can do what you like, so long as everyone knows the procedure."

"So now pretend we have one person searching the bathroom and one watching the other kids," Nicole said.

Ken nodded. "Everyone else needs to start the missing person search in the water."

Jenna listened intently as he explained the search procedure. The head lifeguard remained in charge throughout the search, to make sure the entire area was covered thoroughly and quickly. Ken said the best place to direct operations at their waterfront would be from the dock, since that gave the best vantage point, and he walked out to the end of it himself.

"Under the dock would also be a logical first place to check for a victim," he said. "Kids like to fool around in places like that, but since these planks are less than a foot off the water, no one is likely to stay under there long—unless, of course, they're unconscious."

Jenna shivered again.

"All right. So they're not under the dock," Ken said, continuing his hypothetical scenario. "Time to start a shallow-water line search."

Following Ken's directions, the members of Eight Prime linked arms to form a human chain in order of height from Melanie to Miguel. It took them a couple of minutes to maneuver that way, but soon Melanie was standing in knee-deep water while everyone else walked out farther, creating a line perpendicular to the shore. Miguel ended up in the deepest water, with the ripples lapping nearly to his armpits.

"Remember where you are, so that next time you form up quicker," Ken instructed. "Okay, now, start walking forward slowly, feeling around with your feet."

"Wouldn't you just die if you found a body?" Ben asked Jenna as they waded along, their feet sweeping like metal detectors over unseen mud, rocks, and weeds.

"Don't even think about it," Jenna replied. "I really, really hope we never have to do this for real."

They combed the entire shoreline that way, from one end to the other. Leah stepped into a hole near the far side of the cove and went in over her head, but Jesse and Peter pulled her right up.

"That's good information," Ken said when Leah had stopped sputtering. "It's good to know where your hazards are. All right, now we'll do the deep-water line search, and then we'll be out of here."

The deep-water search was more of the same, only worse. Jenna and Eight Prime formed another line at a depth a little shallower than where Miguel had been standing, but this one was parallel to the shore, facing toward deep water. At Ken's signal, they all surface-dove and swam forward three strokes, feeling their way along the bottom. All Jenna could see was sunlit green water, which immediately turned murky gray with the mud they stirred up. She swam up to the surface wishing she'd brought a mask. Then the line re-formed, backed up enough to overlap passes, and dove again. And again. The water got deeper and, consequently, darker.

On the fifth pass, something in the murk grabbed Jenna's hand. She screamed in fear, momentarily forgetting she was underwater. Her breath was all lost in a mad burst of bubbles, and she swam frantically up toward the sunlight, gasping and choking as she broke through the surface.

"Sorry!" Ben exclaimed, popping up beside her. His blond hair was plastered to his head, making his brown eyes look enormous. "I was just feeling around. I didn't mean to grab you."

Everyone else began surfacing in front of them, having completed their full three strokes.

Jenna felt as if she'd snorted water straight up to her brain. She could sense the headache already forming behind her sinuses, but she had to admit her reaction had been silly.

"Can you imagine if something actually did grab you down there?" she asked, laughing at herself. "I guess I let my imagination run away with me."

"The whole search is a horror show," said Nicole, treading water. "Feeling around in that goo, looking for a body you can't even see . . . I won't tell you what I was imagining."

"Okay, that's enough," Ken called out. "Everyone's tired, and it's getting deep. I don't want to have to rescue one of you, which is part of why the head lifeguard stays up here, by the way. I'm not just directing the search, I'm keeping an eye on all of you."

"Really?" Melanie teased. "I thought you just didn't want to get wet."

The next thing Jenna knew, the entire group was charging out of the water, over the beach, and onto the dock. Ken put up a good struggle, considering it was eight against one, but in the end Jesse and Miguel both grabbed him and jumped. The three of them hit the water with one mammoth splash, followed by the individual splashes of everyone else jumping in behind them.

A water fight ensued, of course. Miguel turned out to be an expert at sending up sheets of water by swinging his forearm across the surface. Melanie and Leah retaliated by turning their backs and flutter kicking in his direction. Jenna squirted Peter with water forced between her front teeth, and he dunked her in return. Everyone was just so relieved to finally have counselor training finished that they all went a little crazy.

"I've got all your certification cards up in the cabin," Ken told them when they eventually straggled onto the shore. "Traci sent your first-aid and

CPR cards with me, and I brought water safety cards too. Just give me a minute to fill them out, and then you can come up and get them."

He took off for the cabin, and everyone else walked up to the flagpole, where their towels and backpacks were waiting. Jenna couldn't wait to get her warm fluffy towel wrapped around her wet body, and most of the others started drying off too. Peter went straight to his backpack, though, took out some papers, and began passing them around.

"This is the counselor schedule for the next couple of weeks," he said. "I'm expecting between thirty and forty campers, so I plan to have at least six of us on at all times. Maybe we won't need that many once we get the hang of it, but I thought it was better to be safe."

"Oops. You have me down next Tuesday," said Miguel. "I think I'm working Tuesday."

"I'll take his shift," said Ben.

"Did you remember cheerleading camp?" Nicole asked, snapping her gum. "Because I just found out when it is, and I'm going to be gone for a whole week."

"I'll cover that, too," Ben offered.

"You can't cover Nicole if you're already on the shift," Peter said. He looked exasperated, and Jenna knew why. He had checked with everyone several times before he'd finalized the schedule.

"Do we have any conflicts for Monday?" he asked.

177

Nobody spoke up.

"No? Then we have a couple of days to work out the problems. Please *recheck* your schedules, then call me tomorrow if you can't take one of these shifts. Pretend this will be our schedule for the second two-week period too, so we can plan a bit farther ahead."

Melanie held up her paper and pointed to the line of bold print across the top. "Is this our name? Camp Clearwater?"

"Unless you guys have a better idea."

"How about Camp Calamine?" Leah quipped, scratching one of her ankles. "Is there such a thing as underwater poison ivy?"

"Don't even say that!" begged Nicole. "You're making me itch all over."

People began stuffing their schedules into their bags and taking off in ones and twos to meet up with Ken in the cabin. Leah and Miguel were the first to go, eager to leave because of commencement and the grad night trip to the amusement park later that evening. Nicole was right behind them, muttering something about an appointment at the hair salon. Melanie and Jesse followed, and eventually Ben, his high-tops dangling from knotted laces draped over his neck. Jenna and Peter stayed behind on the benches, knowing it would take a while for everyone else to get their cards.

"I wonder where Caitlin and David are," Jenna

said, forcing a brush through her hair. "I thought they were going to drive the bus up here for practice."

"Maybe they parked it somewhere," Peter said mischievously.

"Caitlin? Very funny." Although her older sister *had* been unmistakably thrilled to be reunited with Peter's big brother . . . Jenna found herself unable to deny a sudden curiosity. "I mean, I don't think they would. Do you?"

"I wouldn't mind parking it with you."

"Ha!" she said, blushing. "Learn to drive it first."

But walking up to the cabin with her hand tucked in Peter's, she couldn't wipe the smile off her face. And when he pulled her behind the big oak tree for one quick stolen kiss, not only didn't she argue, she almost believed she had thought of it first.

"Are you going to the graduation ceremony tonight?" Melanie asked, hurrying to catch up with Jesse on the path to the parking lot. "It sounds like everyone else is."

Jesse shrugged, a half-smile on his smooth lips. "Leah and Miguel kind of have to."

"Don't tell me you don't want to see your senior friends graduate! What about the guys in football? Aren't the Wildcats losing, like, half the team?"

"I'll be there," Jesse said, "but I'll be sitting with the guys. I didn't know you were all planning to sit together."

"It was kind of a last-minute thing," Melanie admitted, disappointed. So much so, in fact, that she had only just arranged it with the people still left in the cabin, then run down Jesse to try for his answer. The chance to sit with him had been the inspiration behind the whole plan.

"I might see you there, though," he added. "Or at one of the parties afterwards."

"Yeah? Which parties are you going to?"

"Why? Are you making a list?" There was something provocative about the way he said it—as if he half hoped she was.

"I might be."

"Craig Van Houghton's is the main one," he said slowly, searching her face. "I might stop by Cynthia Burke's house first, but only because she begged me. I'll definitely end up at Van Houghton's."

"Definitely?" she teased.

"Definitely."

"All right, then." If it wasn't an outright invitation to meet him, it was close enough. "I might end up there too."

He nodded, his eyes traveling down her body to her midriff. She was still wearing her damp bathing suit, with the addition of hip-hugging shorts. His gaze dropped to her navel, then stopped, fixed as if fascinated.

"Think I should have it pierced?"

"What? Oh. I wasn't looking at *that*," he said, turning scarlet.

Sure you weren't, she thought, amused.

"No! I was just . . . I just . . . You know what? I have a lot of things to do today and I'm just going to go. You have a ride home, right?"

"I can get one," she said, knowing Peter and Jenna were still behind her somewhere.

"Good," he said, not looking at her. "That's . . . good."

Turning around on the trail, he hightailed it to his car.

"Jesse Jones, you surprise me," she murmured, smiling at his back. "For someone who pretends to be so cool, you blush like a little boy."

She sat on a log at the side of the path, waiting for Peter and Jenna to show.

Maybe I'll wear my new halter top tonight, she mused, imagining what color that square of slinky fabric might turn Jesse's cheeks. *Or maybe Tanya wants to go shopping and I can find something really hot.*

Either way, one thing was certain: She'd be seeing him later.

And he'll definitely be seeing me.

Fourteen

"Leah Rosenthal," Principal Kelly intoned solemnly.

Leah walked forward to accept her diploma, ducking her head so that the principal could place the honors ribbon around her neck. She took the small leather diploma case with her left hand, shook the principal's hand with her right, and walked across the small stage to the sound of cheers from the crowd. Turning, she began following the long loop of students back to her seat, then, almost belatedly, switched the tassel on her cap from one side to the other.

It was over.

I'm free. I can't believe it, she thought, numb feet climbing the bleachers to her row. *I can't believe I've actually graduated high school.*

Not that she'd ever thought she wouldn't. But there had been times—plenty of times—when the day-to-day process of getting to graduation had seemed like the longest four years of her life.

"Marti Ross," the principal read.

People cheered for the next girl onstage as Leah inched down the row to her seat. She had spotted her parents in the permanent bleachers earlier, as well as most of Eight Prime, up higher. The group was all sitting together, except for her and Miguel, of course, and Jesse, who was just missing. Peter and Jenna were side by side, hand in hand, looking happy and relaxed. Leah could practically feel the contentment radiating off them at the knowledge that an entire year—the *best* year—still lay before them. They would be seniors, the top of the food chain. They'd be respected. They'd be together.

They'll be out of here so fast it'll make their heads spin.

Reaching her place at last, Leah smoothed the back of her green graduation gown over the dress underneath and sat down, her eyes scanning the rows of students beneath her for Miguel.

If she hadn't learned where he was sitting during rehearsal, it would have been hard to spot him now. From so far above, the gold caps on everyone's heads looked like identical squares. Their brims made it hard to see faces or even hair color. She and Miguel had already exchanged a few smiles during the long speeches that opened the ceremony. Now she concentrated her gaze on the back of his head, willing him to look her way again.

He did, right on cue.

"Congratulations!" he mouthed, grinning. She had signaled the same to him when his row had walked, long before.

The next higher row of bleachers began to empty and refill slowly, its occupants making the long trip down to collect their diplomas, but Leah's eyes stayed glued to Miguel's. Even after he waved and turned back to face the stage, she kept her gaze on him, ignoring everything else. He had called her late that afternoon, just as she and her parents were getting ready to leave for the graduation ceremony.

"Hey!" he'd said excitedly. "Guess what I just got in the mail?"

"I have no idea," she'd answered, experiencing a tickle of excitement herself. As rarely as Miguel used the telephone, it had to be something good.

"My acceptance! From CU. I'm in! Is that perfect timing or what?"

"Perfect," she'd agreed weakly.

"I mean, I was pretty sure I'd get in, but it's such a relief to be positive. My mom is walking around here all weepy . . . I just thought you'd want to know."

"I do. That's great."

Before they'd hung up, they'd made arrangements to meet the instant the ceremony was over so they could head off on the grad night trip together. The school was sponsoring its traditional visit to an amusement park, busing the seniors there and staying all night, and they wanted to get a good seat.

"I'm glad you talked me into going to the amusement park after all," he'd said. "Because I'm in the mood to party tonight!"

Leah had felt vindicated at the time, but now, as the graduation ceremony wound down to its final few minutes, she felt more like crying than partying.

He's going to CU, she thought, depressed. She had once believed she was resigned to that happening, but now she realized that some small, selfish part of her had still been hoping he wouldn't get in, that he'd follow her to California after all. He could get an apartment near her dorm and—

And that's not going to happen, she told herself, swallowing hard. *Deal with it.*

After all, she was the one who was leaving, not him. Miguel *wanted* to go to CU. He wanted to buy a house in town. After he graduated from college, she wouldn't be a bit surprised if he decided to stay in Clearwater Crossing the rest of his life.

In fact, I'll be surprised if he doesn't.

Leah loved her hometown too, but the world was a big place. She didn't want to spend her entire life stuck in one corner of Missouri. She wanted to see new countries, meet new people, think new thoughts. . . .

Did that mean she and Miguel were completely incompatible? That their relationship had no chance?

Elizabeth Zylius crossed the platform—the last

graduating senior. Principal Kelly gave the signal, and the school orchestra launched into the alma mater. The seniors rose en masse, belting out the song one last time. Then suddenly there were caps flying everywhere, cartwheeling gold against a purple-blue evening sky. The crowd applauded; the seniors cheered. People were hugging each other, slapping each other on the back, jumping up and down in the bleachers.

And Leah's weren't the only eyes streaming tears. Not by a long shot.

"I told you you didn't have to dress up!" Guy exclaimed, the moment Nicole opened the Brewsters' front door.

"Thanks. You look nice too," she replied, irritated. After all the rushing around she had done to get ready for his stupid school dance, the least he could do was compliment her.

His eyes looked her up and down. "Did you, uh . . . Did you do something to your hair?"

At least he noticed that, she thought, smiling smugly. The new hairdresser at Mrs. Brewster's salon had done a fabulous job putting in wide platinum streaks around Nicole's face—and if it wasn't the all-over bleach job Nicole had begged for, it was still pretty dramatic. Everyone in Eight Prime had said so at the graduation ceremony that evening.

"It came out good, didn't it?" she said, mollified.

"Well, um, I guess. I liked your hair the way it was before."

"Are you kidding?" Her hair wasn't awful or anything, but she'd been dying for something flashier, and her mom had finally caved. Nicole could barely wait for the rest of the cheerleaders to see her.

"So, are you ready to go, then?" he asked. "You know, if you wanted to, I wouldn't mind waiting while you change into something more comfortable."

She gave him a disbelieving look. "I'm perfectly comfortable."

"Oh."

"Mom! I'm leaving!" Nicole shouted over her shoulder.

Pulling the door shut behind her, she hurried down her walkway toward Guy's car, leaving him to follow. She was already regretting passing up the CCHS parties to be with him, and the way he was acting so far wasn't helping. All the other cheerleaders would be going out that night, and now that Tanya and Angela had started being nicer, maybe she could have hung out with them. It certainly would have done more for her image to be seen partying with the squad than at some geeky Ozarks Prep dance. She opened her own car door and jumped in on the passenger side, buckling up her seat belt before Guy even made it to the driveway.

"Is something wrong?" he asked, letting himself in.

"No."

Just that I spent hours putting this outfit together and you don't even appreciate it, she added to herself as he started the car. She had a new pewter halter top, with spangles that caught the light when she moved, and Courtney had actually come through with the loan of her black leather pants. Nicole's hair was perfect, her makeup sparkled with tiny bits of glitter . . .

He could have said something. Something nice, I mean.

"Do you really want to go to this dance?" she blurted as he pulled out of the driveway.

"I thought I did. Why?"

She didn't meet his eyes. "It's just that there's a lot going on all over tonight. You know, parties and things. And if we don't go to the dance, we can do whatever we want."

Guy nodded as he drove down her street, thinking it over. "And what if we *want* to go to the dance?"

"Well, then, whatever," Nicole said grumpily. "It's your call."

"If you didn't want to go, you should have said so in the first place. I could have made other plans."

"I didn't say I didn't. I just thought maybe you'd rather do something . . . you know. Cool."

"I see. Now that you're a cheerleader, I'm not cool enough for you."

"I didn't say that! Stop putting words in my mouth."

She wished she could get out of the car that

minute. Or better still, that she could travel back in time to the night he had asked her and tell him she'd be busy. There was just no way they were going to have a good time at the dance. Not now.

Guy pulled to the side of the road and stopped. "Look, Nicole, I'm not sure exactly what's wrong with you tonight, but I think we'd better figure it out before we end up in a big group of people."

"What's the matter?" she sneered. "Afraid I'll embarrass you?"

"Actually?"

She didn't let him answer that question. "You're always judging me!" she accused. "It's been that way since I met you."

"I don't know what you're talking—"

"No? Well, how about this? First you tell Jeff that I'm shallow; then you treat me like an insect in Bible class. Finally you decide that maybe, just maybe, you like me—so long as I'm not a model, or a cheerleader, or anything else worth being. You only like me when I fail, because that's the only time I fit into your narrow little world. The instant I step out—"

"That's ridiculous," he interrupted. "I can't believe what I'm hearing."

His dismissal only made her angrier.

"Then what's your problem, Guy? I get all dressed up to go to this thing and—"

"*Over*dressed, you mean. I told you to wear jeans."

"You told me I *could* wear jeans," she corrected,

stunned. "If you don't like how I'm dressed, then maybe you'd better just take me home."

Guy started pulling away from the curb, then stopped, turning to her with a pained expression. "This is the stupidest fight I've ever been in. I didn't say your clothes were *bad*. I just said they're wrong for tonight. You're going to stick out like crazy dressed like that. Things are going to get said. . . ."

"In other words, your friends are all as judgmental as you are."

"Why do you always have to make things so difficult?"

"Just take me home," she said sullenly, crossing her arms.

They hadn't driven far, so the return trip didn't take long. Neither one spoke as Guy pulled back into the driveway he'd left only moments before. The car stopped. Nicole opened her car door, ready to bolt. She had one foot on the pavement when she suddenly turned back around to face him.

"I think it would be better if we don't see each other anymore," she said stiffly. "This just isn't working out."

Guy nodded. "You're right. It isn't."

"I mean, we gave it our best shot and all," she added, a little surprised he was going to let her go so easily.

He nodded again. "We're two completely different people."

"Right. So, uh . . . I guess that's it, then."

"I guess so. See you around, Nicole."

His car was halfway down the street before she fully realized what had happened. Had she really just broken up with him?

And hadn't he taken it kind of well?

For a second, she almost panicked. Guy was leaving—*leaving*—and she'd just told him she didn't want to see him again. Part of her felt like running after the car, like banging on the windows and begging him to stop. . . .

But most of her just felt relieved.

"It's better this way," she said, taking a deep breath. "With cheerleading and everything else on my mind, at least I don't have to worry about that pseudo-relationship anymore."

She let her breath out slowly, letting Guy go along with it. It felt all right. She'd be all right.

Whirling around in the driveway, Nicole charged for her front door.

If I hurry, I can still catch Courtney before she leaves for the parties without me!

"Looking for someone in particular?" Tanya teased.

Melanie jumped, tearing her gaze away from the Van Houghtons' open front door. "I don't look for boys. They look for me," she said, trying for a bored tone of voice.

Tanya laughed. "They're looking tonight, that's for sure. I think half the senior guys wanted back off those buses when they saw you walk by."

"You're exaggerating," Melanie said with a small, satisfied smile.

She *had* caused a ruckus sauntering past the senior buses. Her new flame-orange dress left her entire back exposed, and the front wasn't much less revealing. Matching sandals added three inches to her height and emphasized the tan on her legs. Her blond hair was pinned off her bare shoulders with a few straight strands left framing her face, and her green eyes were heavily lined. Ricky Black had nearly fallen out a bus window, offering to take her to a party instead of going on the trip to the amusement park with his friends.

"I'm willing to make the sacrifice," he'd said, full of mock heroism, "if it will keep you from being alone."

"Oh, Ricky. I couldn't let you do that," she'd said, playing the virtuous heroine in return. "Besides, I won't be alone."

Not much longer, anyway, she thought now, scanning the growing crowd at the biggest party in town. She felt sorry for the seniors, in a way, spending their last night on some lame supervised trip while the rest of the school was living it up. Even Jenna and Peter were at the party somewhere, enjoying the end of the year despite the fact that they didn't drink, or smoke, or get up to half the things already going on in the Van Houghtons' crammed living room.

Then again, neither do I. Anymore.

Melanie sighed impatiently and pushed away from the wall she'd been leaning against. She'd been waiting around for an hour already, trying to look cool while secretly looking for Jesse. She had been sure he'd have shown up by now. She had even dared to believe he'd be as eager to see her as she was to see him. But although people continued to pour into the small house—and out through the back on their way to the keg—she hadn't spotted him yet.

"This is getting dull," she told Tanya. "Maybe we should have gone to Cindy Burke's instead."

"No way." Tanya shook her head. "With all the people showing up here, there can't be anybody there."

Somebody *must be there*, Melanie thought impatiently.

Just then the band started warming up in the backyard.

"Finally!" Melanie exclaimed. "Let's dance."

"Together?"

"Maybe for about two seconds, until the guys start horning in."

Grabbing her friend by the wrist, Melanie pulled her through the crowded house and out onto a small concrete patio. Beyond the concrete, the lawn had been cut short and even, creating one large green dance floor. The yard was huge, with a makeshift platform in one back corner for the garage band that was tuning up. Tiny white lights had been strung across the stage, as well as on nearby trees and bushes, illuminating the band. The other back corner of the lawn was unlit, but the line of people headed into it gave away the location of the beer keg. As Melanie and Tanya stood hesitating at the edge of the patio, the band crashed into its opening number.

Melanie started dancing where she was, not wanting to ruin her spike heels in the grass. Tanya made a few eye-catching moves beside her and, as Melanie had predicted, guys joined them within seconds. Soon people were dancing all around them, on the concrete, on the grass, wherever they happened to be.

This is better, Melanie thought, relaxing just a bit. If she was surrounded by guys when Jesse showed up, it could only make her seem more attractive—and in the meantime, dancing was more fun than standing around. She was dancing to the band's fourth song, which, as far as she could tell, wasn't too different from the first one, when Jesse finally appeared.

She saw him walk out the back door, his chin tilted up like he owned the place. But instead of being irritated by his swagger, as she once would have been, now she found herself smiling. Jesse wasn't that tough, or even that conceited. She finally understood that it was all a façade, an act he put on to confuse the public . . . the same way she put on hers.

She stopped dancing immediately, ready to run to him.

"Back in a minute," she told Tanya.

She had taken only a few steps, though, when she stopped in her tracks, paralyzed.

Jesse wasn't alone.

The unknown girl who came out the back door behind him looked cute and sweet in her simple pink sundress and flat white sandals. A long auburn braid swung down her back, and her eyes were wide and pretty. Melanie watched in horror as Jesse took the girl's hand, watched as the girl smiled shyly in return, watched as they strode through the dancers. . . .

This can't be happening. Who is that? Melanie wondered desperately, backing into the crowd. She didn't want Jesse to see her anymore. Not until she figured out what was going on.

Reaching a dark outside corner of the house, she stepped around it, out of sight. From there she watched surreptitiously as Jesse led the girl onto the lawn near the stage and began dancing with her. They were together; that much was clear. Melanie just couldn't understand why.

Wasn't he flirting with me this afternoon? Or am I totally crazy?

She watched a moment longer, then took a deep breath and rushed back over to Tanya.

"That girl in the pink," she said abruptly, pointing. "Do you know who she is?"

Tanya didn't, but one of the guys in the vicinity turned his head to look.

"Mandi Something-or-other," he volunteered. "Her parents own the convenience store on First."

It's true, then, Melanie thought numbly. *Leah and Miguel were right all along.*

Jesse was seeing someone. He'd moved on.

"Is something the matter?" Tanya asked, reading her expression.

"What? No, not at all. I'm just going to . . . going to . . ."

Melanie pointed toward the house, unable to think of an excuse. All she could think of was getting gone fast, before Jesse saw her and added to her humiliation. She'd have paid any price to suddenly become invisible, but the dress she was wearing drew more attention than a three-alarm fire. She had bought it hoping to make Jesse pant for her. Now, seeing Mandi, she just felt cheap and obvious.

Turning on one spike heel, Melanie hurried across the patio and through the Van Houghtons' back door, then through the crowd and out the front. Cars were still pulling up, dropping off passengers and cruising for places to park. People peppered the front yard and street. Melanie kept her head high as she walked briskly against the flow, her shoes clicking down the front walk.

She was a block away before she let herself stop in the darkness beneath a big, brooding oak, before the tears spilled over and started dissolving her eyeliner. Slipping off her sandals, she started walking again, shoes dangling from one hand. The edge of the road was warm under her bare feet, the stars were bright overhead, and with her pent-up anguish to drive her along, she felt like she could walk all night.

I'm just going home, she thought, brokenhearted. *Tanya will figure it out.*

Fifteen

"Can I have the station wagon?" Jenna asked her mother after lunch on Sunday. "I need to buy some things for camp."

Mrs. Conrad was still washing dishes. "You waited until the last minute. Doesn't camp start tomorrow?"

"Yes, and we're basically ready. I just want to make sure I have enough craft supplies. I'm the art director, you know."

"I know," Mrs. Conrad teased with a smile. "*Everybody* knows."

"Mom!" Jenna squealed. "They do not!"

"Take the car," her mother said, reaching for a dish towel. "Have a good time."

"I won't be gone long," Jenna promised. Grabbing the keys off the hook, she headed for the garage.

Out on the road, she planned her attack.

First I'll go by the copy place and see if they want to donate any paper for the kids to use for coloring. Then I'll stop at the crafts store and get Popsicle sticks. Oh, and pipe cleaners. And glue. On my way home, I'll swing by Fabrictastic and buy some of that cheap yarn.

198

Jenna had spoken to Mrs. Daniels after church that morning, and the veteran Sunday school teacher had given her some great ideas, not least of which was to hit the big yarn sale that weekend and stock up for later.

"You never know when a pom-pom is going to save the day," the older woman had joked. "Kids have fun making those even when you can't think of anything new to do with them."

"I could always let them tie pom-poms on their shoes and pretend they're drum majors," Jenna had said thoughtfully.

"Brilliant!" Mrs. Daniels had exclaimed. "You're going to do just fine."

Jenna smiled as she drove around a corner. She *was* going to do just fine. She'd be the very best art director Camp Clearwater had ever seen.

You'll be the only *one they've ever seen*, she reminded herself, but it didn't take the edge off her good mood.

At the copy place, she had barely begun to explain her errand when the owner gave her two overflowing boxes of white paper that had only been marked on one side.

"Take this with my blessing!" he said, hefting them onto the counter. "I always recycle our mistakes, but in the meantime it's depressing just looking at so much lost income. If your kids want to crayon the blank side, at least this isn't a total waste."

Jenna was loading the boxes into the back of the station wagon when he ran out with a third box.

"Here's some other stuff you might want," he said. "Odds and ends of discontinued colored paper. There's some card stock in there too, and some plastic transparencies that didn't work out for us. Maybe the kids could color them with markers. You know, like stained glass or something."

"That's a good idea!" Jenna said, gratefully accepting the box. In her mind she was already cutting the sheets of plastic into cute shapes for the kids to color and hanging them against windows with loops of the yarn she was about to buy.

The craft store was crowded, and most of the shelves looked as if they'd just come through a major earthquake. By the time Jenna finally found the Popsicle sticks, she was getting anxious to see daylight again. Not only that, but the pipe cleaners were a lot more expensive than she had anticipated.

"Maybe I'll wait," she muttered, balancing an armload of sticks and glue. "I might find those cheaper somewhere else."

Besides, she didn't need them right away. Between the stuff she already had and the yarn she was about to buy, she'd get through the first week of camp with no problems.

Jenna paid for her purchases with the money Peter had given her from the hundred dollars the Eight

Prime guys had earned painting Charlie Johnson's house. Rather than splitting it up, the four of them had decided to donate the whole amount to the camp fund. She made sure to get a receipt for Eight Prime's treasury report, then loaded her shopping bag into the station wagon next to the boxes of paper.

"Whew!" she said, slamming the car door shut and running a hand over her forehead. The mercury had taken a big leap that day, and the hot air shimmered on sticky blacktop. Climbing into the driver's seat, she opened the windows fast and started the air conditioner.

Maybe Peter wants to go swimming at the lake, she thought, heading toward the yarn store. *We could take all this stuff up there and put it in the cabin.*

Although, now that she thought about it, hiking the quarter-mile trail with those heavy boxes of paper didn't sound particularly refreshing.

I'll just stop by and ask anyway. We can always drive the boxes over to the park and put them on the bus for the guys to carry in later.

Jenna felt a thrill of excitement at the thought of the Junior Explorers' bus. She could hardly believe that camp was really starting, and that the bus Eight Prime had worked so hard to earn for the kids would be making the long trip from the park to the lake five days a week, full of cheering, rowdy campers.

It's too bad Caitlin wants to keep her job with Dr. Campbell, or she could be making that ride too— with David. I wonder if they're going to get married?

For someone else that might have been a leap, but Caitlin had been in love with David forever, and there was no question that he was serious about her. They both came from families that believed in marriage—and in waiting for marriage. Jenna could see Caitlin as a housewife so easily, with little girls of her own. . . .

"Oh, no! I passed the street!" she exclaimed, staring into her rearview mirror. "That's what I get for not paying attention."

She had only been to Fabrictastic once, so she wasn't exactly sure how to get there in the first place. Now she was going to have to loop back around and try to find it on the rebound.

"Great," she muttered.

Taking the first right at the edge of town, she started into a residential neighborhood. *If I go down a block or two, then turn right again, I can head back the way I just came and maybe hit it perfectly.*

The problem was, she couldn't find a place to turn right. It seemed that all the side streets in that direction dead-ended into the raised gravel bank that supported the train tracks. She kept going farther out of her way, block by block by block. She had just made up her mind to pull a U-turn and retrace her path exactly when she suddenly realized where she was.

Hey, this is Miguel's neighborhood. Pretty close, anyway.

She considered cruising past his house, then decided against it. He was probably still sleeping in from grad night, and she had things of her own to do anyway.

Oh, wait. This looks like a good place to turn.

The tracks had veered off somewhere, and Jenna made her right turn at last, fairly certain she was on a through street back toward town. If nothing else, she was headed in the right direction again. The houses she passed were old and run-down, not like on her street at all, but the trees were huge and shady and a few of the yards had been mowed. She saw a sycamore in the strip of grass along the sidewalk up ahead with a couple standing under it—no doubt to take advantage of the cooler temperature there. It seemed like a romantic spot. No one else was walking around outside; Jenna's was the only car. The pair stood close together, a dark-haired guy leaning back against the tree trunk, a darker-haired girl leaning nearly up against him. The guy was handsome, even from a distance. Tall, and tan, and . . .

Miguel!

And that is definitely not Leah.

Jenna's heart pounded as she took her foot off the

accelerator. Should she stop? Or should she keep on driving and hope he didn't see her?

Just then, the other girl's head turned and Jenna found herself looking straight into violet eyes.

It's only Sabrina, she realized, feeling her breathing start again. Sabrina Ambrosi and Miguel were just friends.

But so were Miguel and Jenna, and *they* never stood that close.

The station wagon was nearly even with the tree when Sabrina turned back to Miguel, leaned in the last few inches, and kissed him on the mouth.

No!

The car flashed by. Miguel never turned Jenna's way, never saw her at all. But Sabrina had seen her—and recognized her too. Jenna was sure of it.

I can't believe it. I can't believe Miguel would cheat.

Jenna groaned as the consequences flooded over her. *And I really can't believe I had to be the one to catch him.*

Or did Leah already know? Jenna considered the possibility, hopeful for a moment, then reluctantly shook her head.

No way. She'd kill him.

She'd kill him when she found out, that was.

Do I really have to be the one to tell her?

Maybe I should ask Miguel what's going on. Or I could drop a hint to Leah and let her find out on her own. Maybe it's not what it looks like.

Jenna shook her head. *How could that not be what it looked like?*

Pulling to the curb, she took her hands off the wheel, only to find them shaking. She wished with all her heart that she didn't know, that she had never taken that wrong turn. . . .

But now that she'd found out, didn't she have an obligation to do something about it?

If Peter were cheating, I'd definitely want someone to tell me, she thought, turning cold at the mere idea. *And Leah's my friend. Don't I owe her that?*

A shiver passed through her body.

Well, technically Leah and Miguel are both my friends. . . .

But isn't this one of those cases where girls should stick together?

This was a bad, bad idea, Melanie thought, spotting Jesse up ahead in the driveway of the Joneses' Tudor mansion. He was washing his red BMW wearing a pair of cut-off jeans, his bare feet buried by soap suds. She hit the hand brakes on her father's rusty old bike, wincing at the squeal that pierced the quiet Sunday afternoon.

She didn't even know why she had ridden over there. The whole time she'd been opening her protesting garage door, even as she'd wheeled her dad's old bike out into the sunshine, she'd been telling herself that it was okay to ride around, just so long as

205

she didn't end up anywhere near Jesse's house. The last thing she wanted was to see him now, after what had happened the night before.

She still didn't understand what had gone wrong. After he had flirted with her at the lake, after he had practically invited her to meet him at the party, after she had dressed up like a B-movie actress with a walk-on part as a floozy . . . to have him show up with a new girlfriend was the last thing she had expected. The soles of her feet were blistered from walking so far without shoes, and her complexion was still blotchy from all the crying she'd done on the way.

No. The last thing I want today is to run into Jesse Jones, she had told herself.

Except that there he was now, right in front of her.

Melanie froze. Her hands squeezed the handlebars as she hoped he wouldn't see her slumped over the motionless bike, pretending to study something on the ground. She knew she looked ridiculous; she prayed he wasn't looking. Slowly, slowly, eyes still on the pavement, she began to tiptoe the bike around, back the way she'd just come . . .

"Melanie?" He sounded astonished. "Melanie, is that you?"

She froze again, wondering if she should make a dash for it. She heard wet feet padding down the sidewalk toward her, but she could definitely out-distance him on the bike. . . .

Unless he goes back for the car, in which case it's all over.

"Melanie, what are you doing here?" he asked.

It was all over anyway.

"I, uh, I was just out riding around," she said, her eyes now focused on her front wheel.

"Is there something wrong with your bike?" he asked, following her gaze.

"I think it might be the brakes," she said, fastening on the excuse he had offered. "They aren't working very well."

"They're making enough noise. Here, get off," he said, steadying her handlebars.

She climbed reluctantly off the bike, still afraid to look him in the face. Her eyes followed his calves as he pushed the bike up the sidewalk to his driveway. They walked past the BMW, water still beading on gleaming red paint, and into the shade of the open three-car garage.

"I used to be a bike tune-up expert," Jesse bragged, leaning her dad's old junker against a workbench on the wall. "Before I got my car, I mean. I'll bet I can make this thing like new."

She wanted to tell him not to waste his time, that she had a perfectly good mountain bike at home. For reasons that weren't entirely clear to her, though, she preferred her dad's old bone-rattler. She wanted to say that the rust, the squealing brakes, the wobble in the front tire were all part of its charm.

"Okay," she said instead.

Jesse lined up some tools on the workbench, then

began cleaning the front brake with a rag. "So, some parties last night, huh? I can't believe I'm even up this early."

Melanie checked her watch. "It's two o'clock."

"I know," he said, with a grin she didn't want to analyze.

"You stayed out pretty late?" she asked in spite of herself.

"It got light." He picked up a can of something and sprayed part of the brake assembly, then began wiping it again. "What happened to you, anyway? I thought you were going to Van Houghton's party."

"I did."

"I didn't see you."

"I saw you," she said tersely.

He looked up from the bike, crinkled brown brows and confused blue eyes. "What? Why didn't you say hello?"

She rolled her shoulders, not planning to tell him, then suddenly blurted it out. "You didn't tell me you were bringing a date."

He put down the rag. "Mandi? What difference does that make?"

His eyes searched her face. She wanted to look away, found that she couldn't.

"I just think you could have mentioned it, that's all."

"I didn't know I needed your permission," he returned, a slight edge to his voice. "You didn't get mine when you went out with Steve."

"So . . . what? You were trying to pay me back? You invite me to a party you know you're bringing a date to just to make me look stupid?"

Jesse's eyes widened. "Is that what you think happened?"

"What do *you* think happened? I'd heard a rumor that you were into someone, but the way you were acting at the lake—"

"Wait. You heard a *rumor?*" he interrupted, both surprised and irritated. "*How* did you hear a rumor? From who?"

"Does it matter?" Melanie answered wearily. "I just heard you liked some checkout girl at a convenience store and . . . it turns out you do. Right?"

"Why shouldn't I like her? She's nice, and sweet, and—and *normal.* Anyway, for all I knew, you were coming with Steve."

"Steve?" She could feel her eyebrows climb her face. "Why in the world would I be there with Steve?"

Jesse leaned back a bit, less certain. "I thought you were seeing him."

"I broke that off right after the prom! I thought you knew that."

"Why?"

"I thought *everybody* knew that."

"No, why did you break it off?"

Melanie shrugged, trapped. How could she answer?

But Jesse didn't drop it. He walked around the bike to stand directly in front of her. "Why, Melanie?" he repeated.

Her pulse raced like a cornered animal's. She needed an excuse, but what? She stared up into his eyes, so tired of lying, so tired of pride. . . .

"I don't know," she said at last. "I guess he's just . . . not . . . you."

Jesse blinked hard a couple of times. Then he reached out and grabbed her arm. The warmth of his skin melted into hers. She wanted to flow up against him, to feel his heat along her whole body. . . .

"Tell me the truth, Melanie," he demanded, "and no B.S. this time. Are you . . . are you saying that you *like* me?"

"You made it!" Shane exclaimed happily. "I wasn't sure if you'd really come."

I wasn't sure either, Leah thought, smiling weakly. When he had called her earlier that afternoon, asking her to meet him on the CU campus, the first word on her lips had been "no."

Except that she'd never said it. Her parents were both out antiquing, Miguel had said something about hanging out with his family that day, and now that she was fully awake after the long night before, she had to admit she was a little bored. Shane was the perfect cure for that.

"I do have some library books I need to return," she'd admitted cautiously. "What did you want to do?"

"Just hang out. There aren't too many people here for the summer session, and the dorms are practically deserted. I'm getting lonely all by myself."

"Poor baby," she'd replied, making a mental note not to go to his dorm. "I guess I could meet you outside the library. Is the commons open for dinner?"

"You're kidding, right? Like I'm going to eat there if I don't have to? I'll take you to Jay C's. Ever been there?"

"No, but I've heard it's good."

"*Good?* It's barbecue heaven! Meat so tender it melts in your mouth, and the sauce . . ." He had sighed, carried away. "I'd kill to know what they put in that sauce. I would literally commit murder."

"Sure you would," she had laughed.

"Well, okay. But I would twist someone's arm really hard," he'd insisted.

Now, as he ran up to her in front of the college library, he had the same goofy smile on his face she'd so easily envisioned then.

"It's hot out here," she said, pulling the front of her tank top away from her body and fanning it back and forth. Her hair was sticking to the back of her neck, and sweat tickled behind her knees.

"Yeah," he agreed. "Want to get a Coke in a nice air-conditioned building?

"Definitely." She turned her steps toward the commons, but he took her shoulders between his large hands, spinning her in another direction.

"No, this way," he said, loping along at her side. "So how was graduation? Did you have an amazing time?"

She had no idea where they were walking, but his question distracted her for the moment. "Not really. It was kind of disappointing, actually."

"Disap*pointing*?" He looked incredulous. "You graduated, didn't you? What's disappointing about that?"

She shrugged, not wanting to tell him how down she was about Miguel's acceptance by CU, or how stupid and juvenile the grad night trip had seemed compared to her preconceptions. She shook her head a little, especially determined not to mention the way she and Miguel had spent most of the night walking around the crowded amusement park, doing nothing, saying nothing, out of sync with each other. It wasn't as if they'd had another fight—they hadn't—but their thoughts were so clearly on different subjects, so far apart from each other. . . .

"I guess I've been looking forward to graduation for so long that by the time it finally happened I was already past it. You know?" she answered at last. "Like my mind had already moved on, and the actual night was after the fact somehow."

"It's still one hell of a good time," Shane said, grinning.

Leah tried to return his cocky smile, but she was remembering driving Miguel home from the CCHS parking lot at dawn, the top down on her convertible. The cool air had washed over them and a few bold stars had made their presence felt even through the gathering light. The sky had been beautiful, the moment romantic, but in a strange, piercing way that had nearly overcome her with sadness and loss.

I don't know what's the matter with me, she thought, with a sideways glance at Shane. She'd had no idea that graduating was going to make her so emotional. When she looked at the whole thing logically, nothing had really changed. Not really. But she still felt as if she might break down and cry any minute.

"So, where are we going?" she asked, eager to distract herself.

"My dorm. Big vending machines and a nice cool lounge."

Leah's steps faltered. "You did say lounge? I'm not hanging out in your room."

"What's the matter, Little Red Riding Hood?" Shane asked, laughing. "Scared of the Big Bad Wolf?"

Definitely, she thought, giving him what she hoped was a superior look.

She still didn't even know why she was there—except that he'd invited her and for some reason she'd said yes. No matter how nervous he made her sometimes, he seemed to have some sort of power over her. Shane was like one of those thrill rides a girl screams all the way through—then goes on again. He was the lure of the dangerous. And he was darn handsome, too.

"I thought you'd at least want to *see* my dorm room," he persisted. "Since you're going to be living in one next year."

"At a totally different school. They probably aren't the least bit alike."

"They can't be all that different. Dorms are dorms. Way too many people shoved into way too little space. You're going to hate it."

"What makes you say that?" she demanded.

"You're an only child, right? You probably even have a bathroom to yourself. Get ready to shower military style."

"What do you mean, military style?" she asked apprehensively.

"In my suite, the shower is one big curtained-off area with five shower heads in a row. Nothing in between them."

"It is not!" Leah felt queasy just imagining such an appalling invasion of privacy. "Or, anyway, I'm sure the girls' isn't like that."

Shane smiled. "I know a girls' suite that's empty right now. Want to see for yourself?"

Grabbing her by the hand, he dragged her through the lobby doors of a big brick building, straight to an open interior staircase.

"There's the lounge," he said, pointing to a glass-walled ground-floor room as they started to climb. Leah caught just a glimpse of vending machines, broken-down furniture, and a glowing TV in the corner before her toe missed a step and she had to catch the railing.

"I'm not going into some stranger's bathroom," she protested, trying to extract her other hand from Shane's as he continued pulling her up the stairs.

"They don't care. They're not even home."

Leah and Shane reached the fourth floor. "This whole floor is a girls' floor," he said, pulling her down the hall to an entry door. "And I have a bunch of friends in this suite." He opened the door without knocking. "Hello!"

"Shane!" Leah hissed, mortified at the thought of barging into someone's private space.

But a moment later she realized the room he had let them into was simply a small, deserted living area. Five doors in its walls presumably led to the girls' bedrooms. Those were all closed and—Leah fervently hoped—locked.

"See? I told you no one was home." Shane pointed to an open archway to their left. "The bathroom's in there, but I'll wait out here—just in case."

She was glad to know he drew the line somewhere. And she had to admit that she was kind of curious, now that they'd already come so far.

"Just a quick peek," she said, feeling suddenly daring, "and then you owe me the biggest Coke they sell."

She darted into the bathroom: three toilets in stalls, cubbyholes on the wall for soap and shampoo, and one giant shower, exactly as described.

"No way," she breathed, pulling back the curtain and envisioning herself showering in her bathing suit for the next four years. "What a pain!"

Then she ran out of the bathroom, passed Shane in the living room, and kept going, right out the door and into the hall. At least the hallway was public property; no one could get mad at them for being there. Shane followed a moment later, took one look at her face, and started laughing.

"You look like you just robbed a bank," he teased. "Ooh, Mission Impossible! Operation Bathroom is a go! Hey, get it? Go?"

Leah laughed in spite of herself, then gave Shane a push down the empty hallway. "You'd better take me to the Coke machine, mister, before I get rough with you."

Something more than laughter entered Shane's brown eyes. "Really? You promise?"

He caught her by both wrists, pulling her against him before she had a chance to resist. His hands circled around behind her, pinning her arms. They were chest to chest, chin to chin . . . and about to be lip to lip.

"Shane," Leah murmured, wriggling uneasily.

"I've been wanting to kiss you ever since we met," he said, bending his head toward hers.

"No, wait," she said, straining backward.

He stopped. "For what?"

"I just—I don't—This isn't a good idea."

She pulled her wrists out of his hands. He let them go, but his arms stayed looped around her. His embrace wasn't tight. All she had to do was duck out of it and away. . . .

But instead she hesitated, her gaze melting into his. "I mean, it's not because I don't like you. I really like you a lot."

Shane smiled. One of his hands slipped up behind her head, fingers twining in her hair. He held her face in place as his lips moved back toward hers. "Then just relax," he said.

Find out what happens next in Clearwater Crossing #17, *Just Say Yes*.

About the Author

Laura Peyton Roberts is the author of numerous books for young readers, including all the titles in the Clearwater Crossing series. She holds degrees in both English and geology from San Diego State University. A native Californian, Laura lives in San Diego with her husband and two dogs.